Praise for: On Remembering My Friends, My First Job, and My Second-Favorite Weezer CD

An honest and tender look at friendships that question conventional ideas of masculinity. Delgado shows us how the largeness of small kindnesses can last for a long time. This book is a gift of hope. And we don't see these stories often enough, from anyone, but especially from CHamoru people in the continental U.S. (as Delgado makes achingly clear) trying to connect here to a geographical and cultural homeland that has become abstract. This shit is great! It hits on a lot of levels of love not just love between these characters, but also we can tell Delgado wrote these characters with love, which to me means he saw and wrote them as *full humans* with complicated spectrums of being in the world. That's some gracious shit and I appreciate it. And the book is hilarious!

—STEVEN DUNN, 2024 Clay Reynolds Novella Prize Judge, author of *water & power* and *Potted Meat*, and co-author (with Katie Jean Shinkle) of *Tannery Bay*

Masterfully ... carves out a slice of life via SAT ... vocabulary words, a ... burgers, a Weezer CD, gig slinging fast-food ... speculating if this will and friends ritually ... re are be the year The Rock wins ... uzzle certain components of teenag... t, we'll pieces to shape the picture of w... always be. Here, Delgado ... a raucous, gritty, a...

—MICHAEL CHIN, author of *This Year's Ghost* and *Stories Wrestling Can Tell*

More Praise

> Throughout this powerful novella, Delgado crafts a narrative that spirals between the present and the past in order to tell the story of Cody Taitano, a mixed-heritage Native American Pacific Islander and who grew up in upstate New York. His voice drew me in immediately; humorous, self-deprecating, and immersed in pop culture. This story, about memory and manhood, friendship and fatherhood, is an exciting and necessary addition to the canon of Indigenous literature.
>
> —**CRAIG SANTOS PEREZ**, author of the poetry collections: *from unincorporated territory: [saina], [guma], [lukao], [hacha],* and *[åmot]*—Winner of the National Book Award

> In *On Remembering My Friends,* a scratched Pinkerton CD becomes a time machine: We are pulled back into 1999, into the excitement and yearning of teenage friendship, and then volleyed forward once again to see the true weight of these connections. There is danger and uncertainty looming at all times—what happens if a cop stops you, what happens after high school, what happens when the clock strikes midnight, what happens after the pandemic—but there is also such a sweetness here, such a gentle dexterity to Delgado's prose, that you're left with an overwhelming ache of optimism. This is a beautiful book, it will stick with me for a long time.
>
> —**EMILY COSTA**, author of *Girl On Girl* and *Until It Feels Right*

On Remembering My Friends, My First Job, and My Second-Favorite Weezer CD

2024 Winner of The Clay Reynolds Novella Prize

Established in 2001, The Clay Reynolds Novella Prize highlights one book per year that excels in the novella format.

2023 Winner:
Julie Marie Wade, ***The Mary Years***
Selected by Michael Martone

2022 Winner:
Jane V. Blunschi, ***Mon Dieu, Love***
Selected by Renee Gladman

2021 Winner:
Deirdre Danklin, ***Catastrophe***
Selected by Leslie Jill Patterson

For the complete list of winners & to purchase books please visit:
texasreviewpress.org

On Remembering My Friends, My First Job, and My Second-Favorite *Weezer* CD

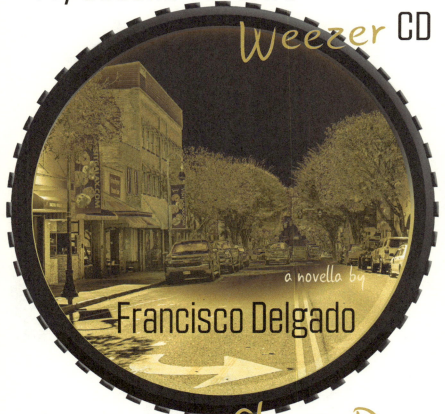

a novella by

Francisco Delgado

Selected by *Steven Dunn*

★trp
The University Press of SHSU
Huntsville, Texas 77341

Copyright © 2025 Francisco Delgado
All Rights Reserved
Library of Congress Cataloging-in-Publication Data

Names: Delgado, Francisco,
Title: On remembering my friends, my first job, and my second-favorite Weezer CD : Winner of the / Francisco Delgado.
Description: Huntsville, Texas : TRP: The University Press of SHSU, 2025. | Includes index.
Identifiers: LCCN 2024043283 (print) | LCCN 2024043284 (ebook) |
ISBN 9781680034189 (trade paperback) | ISBN 9781680034196 (ebook)
Subjects: LCGFT: Novels.
Classification: LCC PS3604.E44388 O5 2025 (print) | LCC PS3604.E44388 (ebook) |
DDC 813/.6—dc23/eng/20241118
LC record available at https://lccn.loc.gov/2024043283
LC ebook record available at https://lccn.loc.gov/2024043284

FIRST EDITION
Front cover design by Happenstance Type-O-Rama
Interior design and graffic art by PJ Carlisle
Author photo courtesy of Riordan Delgado
Printed and bound in the United States of America
First Edition Copyright: 2025
TRP: The University Press of SHSU
Huntsville, Texas 77341
texasreviewpress.org

For Roseanne and Riordan

Contents

1. Lugubrious 1
2. Avidity 11
3. Bemuse 23
4. Aloof 33
5. Constancy 51
6. Reprisal 55
7. Instigate 61
8. Neophyte 69
9. Substantiate 79
10. Assiduous 87
11. Nascent 95

Selective Index 99
About the Author 100

On Remembering My Friends, My First Job, and My Second-Favorite *Weezer* CD

1 Lugubrious

I'M WRITING THIS at the start of a global pandemic, still waiting for a future that was supposed to start twenty years ago. From the other side of 9/11 too, which occurred during my second year of college, and from the flip side of the economic recession of 2008, which hit right as I was old enough to buy a home if I'd chosen a better college major.

Really, what got me started was a broken-in-half Weezer CD my five-year-old son found in my closet during a game of Hide-and-Seek.

"What's this, Dad?" he said, holding it up.

"It used to play music," I answered.

Just seeing the label sparked a memory. This same CD, even back then deeply scratched, on the floor of a friend's old beater in 1999. My friend Nicole—who went on to become my first "maybe-/maybe-not" girlfriend—now only a person I know as an occasional presence, a thumbs-up on my Facebook posts. I reached out and took the pieces in my hand. And in a rush I remembered all our voices, laughing and limitless like voices can be only when you're seventeen.

"Like magic?" my son said.

Earlier today, I wrote a few sentences on a take-out napkin, "We are all living on Facebook now. We keep up with each other—but at a distance."

And now suddenly I've started writing again. I used to write all the time. I used to think I was a good writer, that I might even be famous for it someday. But really, writing was all I had to make sense of the world. How did I forget that?

I'm writing this because of James, who was my best friend

in high school, which means he always will be. Because no one has best friends in adulthood—right? Yesterday, he texted me back that he was doing okay. It was the first time in a year that we'd texted—let alone talked.

I'm writing this because I've lost track of time and of what friendship means, and because during my senior year of high school in 1999, I felt like I was on the cusp of figuring these things out.

These days, I wait for Governor Cuomo's updates, I wait for my students to join me on Zoom, I wait in line—six feet apart from everyone else, eyes to the ground to make sure of my distance—at the grocery store.

Yesterday, outside our local Foodtown, an unmasked man pointed and cackled in my face. "Look at you with that mask! You look *sick*, all of you!"

Here's one thing I know about myself from writing again: other people's perceptions still shape me in every observable way.

Here's another: my whole life, I've only ever wanted one thing: a close group of friends that I could see—and really see myself *in*—whenever I wanted.

*

In 1999, I only saw myself on certain television shows. In professional wrestling, where dudes who kind of looked like my dad and uncles pretended to be cannibals or headshrinkers. Or on shows about cops or hospitals, where people with my brown skin and Wal-Mart clothing were constantly being rushed into interrogation rooms, or rushed off on gurneys where we bled-out or burst from within.

It was the morning of my birthday in early November. First-period Gym class. I'd just taken what I thought was a punch—to the side of my face. My eyes were pressed shut and watering, and all I could pick up on around me was the sound of squeaking shoes and laughter.

One singular laugh persisted. Brian Reece, 6'3", 210 lbs., with

Lugubrious

the musculature and facial hair of a thirty-year-old actor playing a high schooler in a movie.

"Wake up, Taitano," he taunted. Like everyone else in upstate New York he emphasized the wrong syllable in my last name, pronouncing the name as if it was from Italy and not from Guam.

I blamed myself, as I'd been taught to. It was my fault for daydreaming about The Rock and wondering how I, at 5'8 and 100-and-nothing pounds, could someday be like him.

Our classmate, Pete, chuckled and lisped, "Be easy, Brian. Today's Cody's birthday."

Brian and his friends howled and circled around me. As each of them passed through my blurred vision, I met eyes with Dominic Hopkins, the other brown kid at my school. I sometimes thought of Dominic as a Bizarro-world version of myself: who I could be if I was a little richer, with nicer clothes, and straighter teeth, and an imminent sports scholarship.

Pete was laughing loudest of all. He had to throw every ounce of his body into the laugh to make sure Brian could hear him. His hair, permanently in the shape of the bowl-cut he'd had in elementary school, bobbed up and down. Brian and his friends liked Pete because he tried so hard to get in with them.

They serenaded me with a rendition of "Happy Birthday" that some of the other boys, perhaps relieved not to be receiving this kind of attention, joined. Usually, I was invisible at school. But then there were moments like this, which showed me that there were worse fates than being invisible, like being made into a joke.

After school, I watched *TRL* and fantasized about dating a girl who looked like Christina Aguilera. I would have settled for having enough friends to make a whole boyband, though. *Happy Birthday, Cody*—I said to myself, alone in my living room on the wrong side of the state from Times Square—*You beautiful brown son-of-a-bitch.*

James met up with me so we could bike together to work. He showed up at my door holding a single dandelion that looked like it'd been trampled on. It was easy for me to imagine that James had trampled it less out of malice than clumsiness. He probably thought it'd be funny to pass it off as a present. We'd been best friends since fifth grade when some kids and parents at the bus stop tried to get us to fistfight. I liked to think it was sweet revenge that we, the only brown kid and Black kid there, became best friends afterward.

But no one seemed to notice our small act of defiance. Our adolescence just wasn't the stuff of books or movies, which didn't stop us from imagining ourselves as future *WWF* Tag Team champions.

"I heard Brian Reece knocked you out in Gym class," he said.

"How'd you hear of it? That's not even what happened."

"You know how word spreads. So if he didn't knock you out, what happened?"

"He punched me for no reason."

James examined the side of my face nearest him, which was the wrong side. "It doesn't look that bad. A little puffy, that's all. Did you do anything about it?"

"Like what? Punch him back? How do you think that would have ended for me?"

"At least he and his friends would know you weren't a little bitch."

Standing up for myself required a level of confidence I didn't think was possible. Confidence seemed like something that some people were just born with—like the gene for height, or strong cheekbones, or straight teeth. But for other people, like James, confidence was something you had to scrap for. James even learned how to weaponize it whenever anyone tried to take it from him.

There was the woman at the bookstore downtown, who had once accused us of stealing and asked us to empty our pockets, who instead of apologizing, when she was proven wrong, reprimanded us for arousing her suspicions in the first place: "A word of advice," she'd said. "You two should be more mindful of how you carry yourselves. You had your eyes down as you headed to the back. You didn't even say anything when I said hello. That's just ... *rude.*"

James was quick to reply, "We just emptied our pockets for you, even though we didn't have to. Because we're nice, not rude. *You're* the one who's rude. And you're dumb, too. You sell books, bitch, *don't no one want to steal books.*"

James said this last part in a staccato mimicking DMX. An anger and intensity that wasn't his but that he learned to use when others expected it.

The woman banned us "for life," which we found hysterical at the time, but this banishment ended up having a real impact on me because now I had to get all my books at Borders near the mall thirty minutes away. And because I didn't have my license, I had to wait for someone to drive me. Usually it was my sister Heather, who worked at Payless Shoe Source but had worked at a multitude of other stores in the mall before that. Our family joked that she held the record for being fired from the most stores at the mall. We took bets on how long she would last at every job. It embarrassed me to think about my classmates, on their way to American Eagle or Macy's, catching sight of my sister kneeling at the dirty feet of strangers.

James worked at Burger King, where he was hoping to be promoted to Shift Manager. He'd already decided against college, even the community college near where we lived. It was while biking home after visiting James at work (which meant buying one soda and loitering in the lobby) that I'd seen the "Now Hiring" sign at McDonald's and applied. James had tried to get me to work at Burger King with him, but I was making twenty-five cents more an hour at McDonald's. And a part of me liked working someplace where I didn't know anyone, not even James. It was the closest thing to a fresh start that I could get until college.

*

We reached McDonald's first. James biked on while shouting out to me, "Tell Nicole I said 'hi!'" He had developed a crush on Nicole after hearing about how she gave a blowjob to one of my co-workers—

some dude who said he was our age but whose forehead was lined with wrinkles like notebook paper.

"Why do you think about that so much?" I asked him once.

"Because," James smiled, "it means that she *actually does it.*"

I didn't believe the story—or, more accurately, I didn't want to. I liked Nicole because she didn't take shit from any of the guys at work. She and Erin, her best friend, were hired a couple weeks after me, but both of them learned the job a lot faster than I did. At first this bruised my ego because I always thought I was pretty smart. Blame my mom. My whole childhood she called me "the smart one" in the family. She meant it as a compliment, but all it really did was push me away from all of them—like if I didn't figure things out on my own, I had failed them.

At least at work, when I struggled, I could get Erin or Nicole to train me, which meant one-on-one time with them.

"Jesus. What happened to your face?" Todd asked when he saw me. Todd was Assistant Manager. He was only in his late twenties, but he seemed older because he was bald. He was always trying to buddy up to the older guys working in the grill, which meant belittling the younger guys like me working the drive-thru and front counter. I long suspected that Todd chose Employee of the Month based on who he wanted to be friends with, and what they could do for him. My suspicions had been confirmed this month when he selected Jay, whose contribution was selling weed out of the drive-thru window, which honestly did do more for the town than anything I'd ever done.

"I got hit in the face with a basketball," I lied.

Todd looked towards the grill area to make sure he had an audience, "Try catching it next time," he said, when he saw he had one.

I could tell he had more to say, but I cut him off. "Which register is mine?"

"We can't have you up front looking like that. People will think you got in a gang fight. You'll work the grill with Robbie."

Robbie was just finishing his first week, but still needed supervision. I told him where each ingredient was located; the order

Lugubrious

they needed to be placed on the burger. I demonstrated how to wrap up the burger like a perfect little offering to folks whose eyes would, at most, register us as a pair of hands handing them their food.

Erin and Nicole once said that Robbie looked like he could be in NSYNC: he was tall and he had the angular cheekbones and firm jawline necessary for any boyband member. They pestered me until I agreed with them, which started a whole thing where Jay called me "gay" for about a week.

My friend Ben was at the drive-thru window, where he was only tasked with handing food to customers. He was the first friend I'd made there, after he sat with me during break—mostly, I suspect, because he had no one else to sit with. Ben was klutzy, constantly knocking into things and people, so he often worked the drive-thru window where he was less likely to cause chaos. We talked a lot about professional wrestling. And The Rock, whose brown skin and puffy rigid hair matched my own. But Ben and I couldn't talk about anything that night because the drive-thru was so busy. We had to make due with exchanging head nods—until a blonde about our age pulled up in her boyfriend's Dodge Ram.

"Pickles!" Ben screamed, once he'd slid the drive-thru windows closed.

This was code for "pretty girl at the window," which Jay had popularized.

I leaned out of the grill to get a better look, and Robbie, my attentive trainee, followed my lead. Todd yelled at us to get back to work—after he took a quick look for himself.

"Ew, Todd!" Nicole said. "Why you looking at underage girls?"

My shift ended at the same time as Erin's and Nicole's, at nine o'clock. We were replaced by students from the community college—dudes in their early- to mid-twenties who seemed so worldly to me at the time. They drove Jeeps and listened to Sublime. Typically they ignored me. They always smiled at Erin and Nicole, though.

Jay, whose car was known for its Insane Clown Posse decal, and who knew Dominic Hopkins (Bizarro-World Me) "from around," was the only one to ever greet me. And when he did, he made such a show of it because he knew the attention would embarrass me. "Hey, Player B, what's up, man? How's life? You getting any?" he shouted. He spread his arms out wide, like a wrestler making his grand entrance, right underneath his Employee-of-the-Month plaque.

 Me: Player B to Dominic's Player A. It was stupid but, like a lot of dumb things, it got people laughing so they never forgot it.

 "Want a ride home, Player B?" Nicole teased.

 "Why? Is it because it's my birthday?" I asked. There was definitely a more natural way for me to tell her, but I couldn't think of it. And this did succeed in getting Nicole to wish me happy birthday, which was all I wanted.

 "Whose birthday is it?" Jay asked, a smirk already forming on his lips. No one heard him but me, and there was no way I was going to tell him.

 "Todd told us you tripped downstairs at your school? You can't even tell," Nicole said.

 "That's not what happened," I said. "I fell off my bike."

 "Let me give you a ride, then. To help keep you safe. It could be my birthday present to you!"

 I declined because I was worried that I might smell too much of the job we were all leaving. And I really liked biking around Canandaigua because it was just about the only way I felt a part of it—moving through it at my own leisure, limited only by my choice in direction. Wind blowing off the lake felt good on my back, ridding me of the smell of French-fry grease and burger smoke. Biking around at top speed, I was more than my life at school. I was all possibility.

✳

Canandaigua has two major roads: Main Street, which cuts from north to south towards the lake, and Route 5 & 20 that goes east to west. I imagined that from above, the town resembled a line graph, structured and self-contained. This straightforward layout of the

Lugubrious

town made it pretty difficult to get lost: you always knew exactly where you were—or, where you were trapped.

I took Main Street home because I liked how, if I followed it far enough, it would take me to the thruway and the thruway could take me anywhere. I would often trace I-90 on the map and marvel at how far it could take me: not quite to my family in California or all the way back to Guam, but at least to Ohio, which my Seneca grandma taught me meant "good river," but the word could've just as easily meant heaven, just by virtue of its elsewhere-ness. Nicole honked at me from her yellow Honda Civic as she passed. I could only make her out by her silhouette: her aquiline nose and angular chin, her narrow shoulders.

I thought of the word "lugubrious," which I'd learned from my SAT prep, and that's what I was thinking about when I saw flashing lights behind me. I turned and saw the cop car and stopped. I got off my bike. It hurt my eyes when I looked back into the headlights, but I didn't look away or look down.

Two officers approached. They were about the same height: maybe six feet tall, if not an inch or so more. They had the same haircut: buzzed on the sides and back, the top combed forward to a spiky front. One looked leaner than the other, but that changed depending on how the streetlight struck them. One looked taller than the other, but that could have been the result of how quickly my eyes vacillated between them.

"Hello," said one officer.

I said it back, because I felt I had to.

"Where you coming from?" he asked.

"Work."

"Where at?" the other asked.

"McDonald's." They made me repeat myself.

"Til when?"

"I got off at nine," I said. "I left a little after. Maybe 9:10."

I felt the need to account for every minute of my night. My dad, a US Army Sergeant, had taught me to respect all people in uniform. He also taught me to side with people suspicious of me.

One of the officers hurried back to the car when the radio sounded. The other waited with me. I stayed put without having to be told. I would have thought that the officer nearest me would be tasked with chasing me if I tried to get away, but (like most cops in our sleepy-ass town) he didn't look like the running type. His eyes followed his partner as if waiting to be told what to do next. When he finally did look at me, it was just to tell me I should be wearing a helmet.

The other officer returned, "It's not him. Let's go." Already turning away to forget all about me, he explained, "You matched a description, is all."

Overheard on the radio, a voice iterated: "Young male, Hispanic. About 5'11". Wearing a hat. On a blue bike."

I'd been called Hispanic—or some slur related to it—many times in Canandaigua. But this was the first time that it led to more than hurt feelings, and I was still too young to realize how much worse it could have gotten.

At home, I thought of how I could tell people about what had just happened. I'd have to make a joke about passing for 5'11". The joke would be easier to handle if I made it first. At the very least, it would save me from having to talk about racism, which took me years to get comfortable doing—and sometimes, even still, I don't do it well.

2 Avidity

THE FOLLOWING MORNING I raced downstairs to catch the news. I wanted to find out what the cops were up to. I had no delusions of being mentioned; long ago I'd learned I wasn't that important.

Dad was already awake, ironing his clothes with the news on. For a moment I thought about retreating upstairs and waiting for Heather or my mom to wake up. I even pivoted on my heel to head back up to my room, but I was betrayed by a creaking stair.

The television flashed overhead shots of the traffic that awaited Mom and Dad on their ride to Rochester, where they worked at the VA. It was Dad's first job after leaving the military, and from the way he spoke about co-workers and patients (all "dumbasses") I knew that it would become his first of many.

"Hey, do you go to school with a Dominic Hopkins?" he said. Something about hearing Dominic's name from Dad's mouth made it sound new, like worlds crossing over. Like when Urkel showed up on *Step by Step* to teach everyone how to dance, or when Chris Jericho appeared on *Monday Night Raw* that summer. "The police were chasing him last night. They finally got him this morning."

"For what?"

"Selling drugs. You ever buy from him?"

I could never tell if Dad was being serious or just messing with me, so I would never answer right away.

"I'm kidding, man," he said, "You gotta relax and learn how to take a joke."

I mentioned being stopped by the cops on my way home from work. I wasn't trying to suggest anything, but there was a part of me that believed my encounter with the cops and Dominic's arrest were related. I was hoping Dad would say it, because I'd believe it more coming from him. But instead, Dad rolled his eyes and slammed the iron down.

"What do you mean? Because of your skin color? What have I told you about thinking that shit? You got to stop making everything about that."

"What else do I make about it?" I went to ask. I don't know how many words I got out before Dad interrupted me, but I know the number of words he'd heard was zero.

"You know something?" he asked (usually when he thought I didn't), "I was the only brown person, minority, *whatever*, when I left Guam for boot camp. Did it stop me? No. I just minded my own business, kept working, and I was fine."

When he was stationed in Germany, Dad had met Uncle Tony, who had introduced him to Mom. Uncle Tony and Dad had bonded quickly over the fact that both their families were from Guam, so I wanted to point out: our culture and race sometimes *did* count for something. But I worried he'd call me a smartass—or a dumbass.

"They asked me a few questions, and I answered them, then they let me go," I said.

"Did they ask you anything to make you think that they were being racist?"

My silence was all Dad needed as proof that he was right. He left me in the living room without saying a word, which was how a lot of our conversations ended back then.

*

At school, all anyone could talk about was Dominic. Classmates competed over who knew more, who saw him last. I didn't get too caught up in it because I was more concerned with getting through the day, which would be easier *without* P.E. (and Brian) and *with* SAT prep (where I actually had a few people to sit with).

I met up with James before Pre-Calc, the only time we saw each other during the school day. He was on his way to BOCES, where he was taking classes to be a chef but really where he spent his time flirting with girls from other school districts. He would sometimes use this as proof that he was worldlier than I was, more knowledgeable, and I couldn't really argue.

"Did you hear about Dominic Hopkins?" I asked.

"Of course, dude. Everyone's talking about it. *Wha? Cuz I'm not AP like you, I gotta be stupid?*"

I didn't judge him for sometimes slipping into that style of speech—*talking ghetto*, as others called it—because I understood that it was James's way of having fun with people's racist expectations of him. But for me, as a non-descript brown kid who seemed to pass for everything from Asian to South American, I had no clear expectations to meet, no speech to emulate. Just the same words that always failed me—that is, until I remembered I had something to say for once. "I got stopped by the cops biking home last night," and when James didn't interrupt me like he often did, I finished my story without embellishing.

"I wonder why Nicole and Erin were heading uptown," he said. "You should ask them next time you see them. But make it sound casual."

I was about to get pissed at him for missing the point when James continued—

"So you think that the cops stopped you because they were looking for Dominic? Like, they thought you were him?"

I was glad to hear someone else say it. "What do you think?"

"Probably. People here are always saying that minorities look the same, and when you call them out for it, they always say they're joking. But really, they mean it."

"We're not even close to the same. Dominic's part Puerto Rican," I said.

"Like that matters," James replied right before the bell.

*

On Remembering My Friends, My First Job, and My Second-Favorite Weezer CD

My Pre-Calc teacher started class by giving us "the opportunity to discuss our thoughts and feelings." Most of us had already been doing that in the hallways, so at this point we were bored at the prospect of sharing our feelings again—or, more accurately, having to listen to other people's.

"I bet he's doing this because he didn't plan anything," a classmate whispered.

"The teachers keep acting like Dominic's arrest is some kind of Columbine," someone else quipped.

By the end of the day, my own small involvement in Dominic's saga had spread. This was probably because of James, who people liked to hear talk, even though they ridiculed him about "running his mouth too much."

It got back to me on my way to my SAT prep course. Andrew and Eric, friends of mine from Cross Country, eagerly asked if what they'd heard was true. They giggled in excitement when I confirmed. Actually, since last year, I'd only hung out with them when circumstances necessitated it. Bus trips for races. On weekends when we would happen to be placed in the same group for some assignment. My mom thought that the three of us were really close though. I'd once told her I didn't really like Cross Country. When she asked why I kept doing it, she answered her own question with, "It's because your best friends do it, isn't it?" I nodded because she always seemed to need to hear that I had friends at school besides James. She just wanted me to be happy, but I wished I could tell her how exhausting it was to have to make my life at school seem better so she could feel good.

We all trekked upstairs together to the computer lab where the prep class met, and grabbed a row of seats at the back of the room, far away from the instructor who we recognized as Mrs. Long's longtime substitute—when she was killed by her husband in a murder-suicide our freshman year.

We were waiting for Megan, who was also on the Cross Country team. We'd all been friends since middle school—except for the three or fourth months sophomore year when Megan dated a senior who taught her about Pink Floyd and smoking weed. As the only girl of the group, Megan could bring us together and drive us apart without even trying.

Megan arrived right before the class started. She smiled wide and waved, each of us believing that the wave was mostly ours. Now that we were all together, I noticed that I was the only person in the group not wearing a shirt from a Cross Country Invitational—partly because I was no longer on the team but also because I never finished high enough in the rankings to get a shirt, which would only go to the top 20 or 25.

Part of the reason I'd stopped running Cross Country was because I didn't see the point in devoting so much time to something that wouldn't ever help me pay for college. I wasn't a standout runner—just fast for my gym class. I was never going to get a college scholarship, which is what I really needed.

In hushed voices (so as to not disrupt the instructor) Andrew and Eric took turns telling Megan about my encounter with the police, how close I was to being arrested instead of Dominic, which wasn't really true. I wanted to jump in and tell the story for myself, but I loved how Megan looked at me every now and then as she listened.

"Were you scared?" she asked.

"No."

Immediately Andrew and Eric called me out for lying until we were all shushed by the instructor. Usually I hated it when kids in class would disrupt the teacher, but it was different to actually be a part of it for once.

SAT Prep ended, as always, with a practice exam, and that day we were practicing the verbal portion of the test. Of the group I got the second-highest score—Megan, the first—and I was happy that my score would spare me the teasing that could make me lose standing with Megan. Teasing that, soon enough, was directed at Eric (who'd scored the lowest) by Andrew (who'd scored the second lowest).

On Remembering My Friends, My First Job, and My Second-Favorite Weezer CD

"Thought all Asians were supposed to be smart," Andrew said, "How'd you score so low?"

"English is my weak spot," Eric explained, trying to regain status with Megan.

Eric got teased a lot for being Asian. One or two times I'd joined in to deflect attention from myself. I would tell myself it was all right because of all the other times when I stood up for Eric and told people to stop.

I was the only one in the group taking the test on Saturday. I wasn't worried because I always felt destined to get a high score on the SAT. Even hearing about it in middle school I felt anticipation instead of nervousness. Like, when I took the test it was going to prove things I only suspected about myself: how smart and talented I really was, how special.

This was the movie narrative that played in my mind: I was a "Free Lunch" kid who, rather than give my name to the lunch lady and expose myself as poor, often skipped lunch and hid in the library. In this fantasy movie version, the only appropriate ending was a perfect SAT score and leaving for my top-choice college, which at that point was NYU because I kept seeing it and hearing about it on TV shows and in real movies.

"NYU?!" James had laughed (the only time I mentioned it to him), "Damn, dude, you really want to be in one of those white-people movies, don't you?" It was scary how well he knew me—the way I saw myself in my head.

I could also see myself heading to California, where I had family on Dad's side, and James had laughed that off too, "Man, California is so boring."

"Is there anything that isn't boring to you?" I snapped.

"Girls."

I fantasized about doing so well on the SATs that Megan might ask me to come to her house to tutor her. Just the two of us.

Alone in her room.

"Good luck on Saturday," Megan said. "You'll do well. You're smart."

"When are you taking yours again?" I asked, as if I didn't remember. I wanted to engage her without Eric and Andrew getting in the way.

"January," she said.

"That doesn't give you much time to improve your score if you need to," Andrew jumped in. "You're not worried about bombing the exam and getting stuck with a low score?"

"I don't put so much weight on the SATs. And truthfully, I don't want to go to a school that does either."

"What schools are you applying to?" Eric joined in.

"Mostly SUNY schools. Geneseo. Buffalo. I really like the idea of attending a public school."

"But what's your dream school?" Eric pressed.

"NYU?" Andrew offered. He slapped my thigh and smiled when he said it, and I wanted to punch his face in.

"Cornell," she said, and her eyes beamed when she said it, "I don't want too many people to know in case I don't get in."

"I can see you going to Cornell," I said.

And Eric and Andrew agreed right away, so that what would have been her "Thank you" only to me became a "Thank You" to all of us instead. She did *look* only at me though afterwards adding, "By the way, your face looks pretty healed. You can't even tell Brian beat you up."

I thought of all the words we'd learned that meant to make something less severe: *alleviate, assuage, palliate, mollify, mitigate,* and *lenify*. I assessed my days by how many new words I learned. Studying for the SATs seemed like the only thing giving my life structure.

*

After Prep Class I biked to McDonald's to see who was working. It was a new, exciting feeling for me to be able to go from one group of friends to another. And while I thought it was a shame that I didn't achieve it until senior year, I was so sure I'd have it again in college.

And many more times, for the rest of my life.

The lobby at McDonald's was a mess. Trash containers overflowing, a lingering frenzy in the air from the dinner rush. Todd was at the drive-thru window assembling orders, too busy to see me. I cut through the tables, sticky with dried ketchup and splattered barbecue sauce, until I made it to the front registers where Nicole and Erin were standing.

"What are you doing here?" Nicole asked.

"Just wanted to see what you were all up to."

"Wait," Erin said, "you showed up even though you're not scheduled? Weird."

"I was already down here on my bike. No big deal."

Erin was wearing a necklace with a heart-shaped pendant. She was twirling it with her fingers and looking past me as I was talking to her. I turned to Nicole, who asked if I could take her day shift on Saturday.

"Sorry. I've got the SATs," I said.

Nicole grimaced (I thought because we wouldn't be working together) and said, "I'm having a party and I wanted to use the afternoon to get ready."

"You're throwing a party?" I said.

"You should come, Cody. You and James, both! Do you guys go to parties? I've never seen you at one."

I liked that she'd assumed we didn't party because she'd never seen us at one, and not that we'd simply never been invited.

"Were you guys heading uptown last night?" I said. "I thought I saw your car."

"You may have," said Nicole. "We were going to a friend's. You know Dominic Hopkins, don't you?"

I laughed without meaning to. They looked at me, confused, Nicole furrowing her brow.

I wanted to tell them everything that happened last night after work, but I worried I would sound like I was horning in on their friend group. I kept it simple instead. "I actually got stopped by the cops on my way home because they thought I was him." And I repeated the police description I'd heard over the cruiser's radio.

"They thought that *you* looked like Dominic?" Erin said.

"They said I matched a description," I explained. "They asked me a few questions and let me go."

Erin looked at me like a math problem. Numbers that would never add up.

"I can see the resemblance, actually," Nicole said.

"We're about the same height," I joked. But neither of them got it.

"So were you heading to his house too?" Nicole asked. "You should have caught a ride with us."

"Next time."

I took a seat at a table when the next customer came in. I wondered if Nicole already knew Dominic had been arrested. I decided she must have, or she'd have asked more questions. A few of my classmates came and went. I recognized them by their Abercrombie clothing, their necklaces and rings from Aeropostale and Pacsun. I'd served many of them before. Each time they pretended they were seeing me there for the first time. But maybe that's how it was for them. Seeing me in my uniform—just another lowly McDonald's worker, only there to take their order and retrieve it—probably matched their perceptions of me better than when they saw me tutoring them, and they had to contend with the fact that maybe there was more to me than being poor and ignorable.

Erin joined me during her break. She ran her fingers through her hair and shook out dandruff on the table and blew it in my direction.

"Thanks," I said, dusting myself off.

"I hate how this place makes me smell. I have to put my clothes in the washer twice to get the smell of hamburger meat off me. My mom says she's going to make me pitch in on the water bill if I keep doing that."

"You do kind of smell, though," I said, and she shoved my shoulder.

"Did you hear about Ben? He got fired. This was his third time missing his shift."

I'd once heard Ben explain to Todd how hard it was for him to get a ride. How his brother had moved and taken their Toyota and how his Dad was "between cars." His Mom worked long hours at a nursing home so she couldn't take him either. While it all seemed plausible to me, Todd was not understanding, stating bluntly, "Then stop taking shifts you can't show up for."

"That's too bad. I liked Ben," I said to Erin.

"He was all right. Kind of a goof, though. Always screaming, 'Pickles! Pickles!,' like an idiot."

I playfully took offense. "What does that mean? Am I a goof then too?"

"Absolutely. All of you are." She paused to look at me. "Hey, were you *really* going to Dominic's party? Dom says he doesn't know you."

"You asked about me?"

"Not directly. When I first met him, he asked if I knew anyone he went to school with. I swear when I mentioned your name he didn't know who you were. I don't know ... maybe I *didn't* mention you though? I can't remember."

I figured I thought more about her and Nicole than they did about me. I didn't think of myself as someone people thought about when I wasn't around. But I wanted to change that. Nicole's party felt like a start. Her party was all I thought about that day. Not the SATs, not Dominic Hopkins, not anything else. Just the party, my first ever.

✷

And now I'm thinking about parties again. My son's sixth birthday is here. Friends should be gathering to celebrate him—all of us at some indoor labyrinth of a playground. Pizza and chocolate cake, a table of his Kindergarten classmates. But everyone is "sticking to their pods" and "sheltering in place."

Avidity

He accepts our homemade pizza and store-bought cake. He tears open his box of Legos, and I spend all day with him, building homes and bridges on the living room floor then knocking them down. The two of us giggling, just as I imagined he and his friends would have done. I make a good enough substitute.

3 Bemuse

THE NEXT DAY at school I told James about the party. Actually, how I put it was probably like: "Nicole invited me to her party on Saturday. You should come with me," because I wanted to seem a little important to someone, particularly a girl, for the first time.

I also told him about Ben getting fired.

"The nerdy kid?" James said.

"I liked him. You don't have to call him a nerd."

James shrugged, the closest thing to an apology any of us were capable of. "Nicole's party should be fun."

"Do you want to bike there?"

"We'll be really cool arriving on our bikes, won't we?" James mocked. "I can borrow my neighbor, Will's, car. He won't mind. He owes me because I hid his drugs once while his probation officer visited."

"He's going to let you drive his car? But you just passed your road test. Have you even gotten your license yet?"

"It's coming. And why wouldn't Will let me drive the car? He said he's going to sell it to me."

The prospect of James getting Will's car seemed similar to those promised vacations to Six Flags from his mom every summer, or those birthday phone calls from his dad. I didn't want James to get his hopes up. But I also didn't want to be the one to destroy them.

Thoughts about Nicole's party got me through the whole day, even ninth-period Study Hall, which I originally planned to use to study for the SATs. Instead, I re-read passages from *1984* because it was in a library cart next to me. I mainly remembered the book for putting me to sleep until I got to the point when Julia tells Winston that she loves him. It didn't hit me the same re-reading, now that I saw her confession coming—and knew how their story ended.

Temporalize, to procrastinate.

Sanguine, optimistic.

Thinking about the party even got me through walking home in the rain. I was halfway there, still deciding about which shirt I should wear later to Nicole's party, when a car stopped beside me, a Mitsubishi, metallic-silver, brand new.

"Need a ride, man?"

I peered in and saw Brian Reese, my gym-class bully, as giant as ever. "Let me at least take you down the road," he said.

All evidence from my life told me not to take the ride, but I took it because high-school movies actually had me believing this could be the scene where Brian would apologize, and the two of us would arrive at a mutual respect.

Brian was in-no-small-part responsible for my desire to go far away for college. Even before the birthday punch, Brian had: shoulder-blocked me in the hallway; knocked the books from my hands; and one time during freshman year he'd tossed a gym sock onto me as I walked by him in the hallway. I was halfway to class before his girlfriend ran up behind me and removed the sock from my shoulder. "Sorry about that, Cody," she said, repressing her own smile. I'd known right away when Brian had done it. I couldn't acknowledge it though, because then I would have had to remove it. If I removed it, it would create the very kind of spectacle that Brian wanted, because then I would be left with only two options:
1) Call them "Assholes," which they would take as a compliment; or 2) Lunge at them swinging (and get my head kicked in); so I went with option 3) Pretend not to notice. Playing dumb had its benefits. But I was already starting to wonder, how long could I play dumb before people just thought I *was* dumb?

I got in the car, and we sat in silence. Brian reached the end of the road and offered to take me the rest of the way. "Where do you live?"

"Camelot." The name had connotations of high royalty, of romance, and heroism, but the Camelot in Canandaigua was an apartment complex whose biggest appeal was the free cable. I liked it because it was home. And at least it wasn't far from James's apartment complex. I decided to be heroic and pushed on, "So, have you heard from Dominic?"

"Why? Have you?" Brian replied.

I wasn't sure what Brian had heard from people at school—if the news about me being mistaken for Dominic had reached him, and what he might feel about it. "Honestly, I haven't spoken to him since middle school," I said.

"Well at least you're not one of those kids on the news, acting like you knew him." All his CDs tumbled out of the sleeve strapped around the visor when Brian took a turn too quickly. I rushed to pick them up. And right away I hated myself for doing so. But I was already hunched over ("assed up," as James would say) in the passenger seat of the car, driven by the kid who had punched me on my birthday, by the time I realized what I was doing. I remember thinking that there were only two ways I could make us friends after all this: Stand up for myself and confront Brian, as Dad and James would suggest, or endear myself to him by being super friendly.

"You didn't have to do that," Brian said, instead of *Thanks*.

Brian's car stereo was connected to his CD player by an adapter, which was something I definitely planned on buying whenever I got my own car. I'd recognized Weezer's *Pinkerton* immediately when I got in. Now I thought about using it to generate conversation, but in the end I chose to enjoy the songs by myself, and was humming along with "El Scorcho" when Brian explained, "I only got this CD because my parents went to FYE and asked for a recommendation for *alternative music*, as they probably put it. I was pissed, but... I don't know, it's okay."

"'Butterfly' is *really* good." The vulnerability of the vocals, the stripped down acoustic guitar. It spoke to me, and made me believe I understood the lyrics about using someone for sex, when I hadn't even been on a date yet.

He grimaced. "No, that song sucks. What other bands do you listen to?"

I took my time answering, worried I might say another band he didn't like, but then Brian pulled in front of my townhouse. He gave it a quick once-over before looking back at the way we'd come, his only way out.

"Thanks for the ride," I said as I exited.

"Yeah, sure. See you at school tomorrow."

And he said it like something had changed between us, like he might actually say "*Hi!*" next time he saw me, but the two times we passed each other in school the next day, he gave no indication that anything was different.

"Maybe he thought he was giving a ride to Dominic, since you two look so much alike," James teased when I brought it up.

"Well. Dominic and I *are* about the same height," I said, determined to pull off the joke with someone.

"What? Are you stupid? You and Dominic are *not* the same height, dude."

In Study Hall I reviewed for the SATs. A few minutes into studying though, I thought back to the *last* time Brian and I were cool with each other: fourth grade, when we worked on a model of the solar system together. While I did most of the work on the assembly, Brian had stepped in during our class presentation when I went to speak . . . and went to speak again . . . and nothing came out. . . . He saved the day. We called it even.

This memory triggered another from seventh grade when Brian had made it a point to tell me that I wasn't invited to his birthday party at his family's lakeshore cottage. He'd done it in front of everyone in homeroom. Sometimes I looked back at this as the moment when my social status was cemented because Brian had humiliated me so publicly, and because I'd allowed it.

✱

Bemuse

Bemuse: to confuse someone.

After Study Hall, I met with my guidance counselor Mr. Greer. He'd taken over students with last names beginning with T–Z after Ms. Schmidt died in a car accident that got the whole town chittering for about a week. I can't even remember Ms. Schmidt, having only met her one time as a freshman when she wanted to know more about my academic interests.

Mr. Greer was tall and lean like a running coach, with the same no-nonsense demeanor. The type of adult who did not care about your struggles—unless you could sublimate them in your college essay. His office wall was filled with pictures of his lacrosse days at Dartmouth. We only started meeting this year because I was a graduating senior, and he needed to check in on my progress applying for college and financial aid.

"Have you started your personal statement?"

I shook my head—a response he clearly expected.

"You'll need one for your applications, Cody. Schools are going to want to know why they should admit you. You won't come with a sports scholarship, unless that has changed? It hasn't? Okay, and you won't necessarily have an academic scholarship, either. So you need to have a really strong statement to go along with your transcript."

"What should I say?"

He looked away from me, so I couldn't see the full roll of his eyes. I appreciated it when people tried to hide their complete disdain at having to talk to me.

"Didn't you say your dad is from Guam? Maybe you can write about that family history of yours. You can talk about what it means to you to be ... *Guamese?*"

"Guamanian," I said. "Chamorro, actually."

"Right, right," Mr. Greer replied, waving me off. "How about you write something—a few hundred words or so, not much—for us to review together in our next meeting?"

"Okay," I answered, keeping intact my streak of short responses.

"Good," he replied, maybe mocking me.

I got up to leave when I sensed our meeting was over. But I stopped right at the door. "Do I have to write about cultural identity?" I asked.

He dropped his pen, which he really wasn't using anyway, except in his performance of reviewing something on his desk. "Well. What *else* would you write about?"

"I work at McDonald's after school. What if I become Employee of the Month?"

"Working at McDonald's might not be the accomplishment you think it is." And he ushered me out with more words reiterating what I *should* write about.

It was hard for me to think about accomplishments or identity—even harder to *write* about it. What identity could I claim, or what had I done that would make anyone want to claim me?

At home after school I caught my sister Heather on her way out the door. She was headed to work, as she often was, and today was one of the times I got a ride to the mall from her.

We made it in about 30 minutes, which was typical of her. And kind of impressive, considering she was driving a fifteen-year-old Omni that couldn't handle the thruway.

When we arrived, Heather headed straight to Payless. I followed her most of the way, a few steps behind, just to see if her co-worker Jennifer was there. Jennifer had a nose ring and purple highlights in her hair—too cool for most of us in upstate New York—and a moon tattoo on the top of her foot, which I used as my excuse when she and Heather caught me staring once.

"I was admiring your tattoo," I'd said.

"Do pictures of moons...*excite* you?" Jennifer replied, making me squirm.

Recently, I'd finally conjured the courage to speak to her. Heather was helping a customer and "99 Luftballoons" started playing on the radio. Jennifer commented that she loved this song— "even though I don't know what she's saying," she added. And I tried to impress her by translating the first line ("Do you have any time for me?").

"Jennifer's not here today, Cody," Heather said. "You don't have to hang around." The last thing she wanted was me hanging around. My leaving freed her to flirt with her manager, a senior at St. John Fisher College where she was a sophomore.

I chose a direction at random and headed off alone. I stopped in a few clothing stores. American Eagle. Abercrombie & Fitch. Structure. I recognized a choker necklace many of the girls at school wore—specifically Megan, whose collarbone raised it just a couple precious centimeters higher than the rest. I was staring at it once during Global Studies when she turned to me and commented, "You smell funny today," which I tried to diffuse by explaining that I'd just gotten out of Bio where we'd dissected a pig fetus.

Next I walked the aisles of FYE. Doing so always helped me see that there was so much world beyond my hometown and my high school—so many people out there that I could maybe connect with someday. I stopped in front of the CDs of my favorite bands—Nine Inch Nails, Radiohead, Counting Crows—and felt an odd sense of accomplishment because I owned all the CDs that FYE carried, and even some they didn't.

I even owned all the Smashing Pumpkins CDs they had—including *Adore*, which I bought out of loyalty. Back then I was loyal to bands the way other people were loyal to sports teams.

Eventually I circled back to Payless and waited for Heather. Through the front windows I watched her count the register and turn out the lights. Just as the store went dark, her manager wrapped one arm around her waist and pulled her into him, the two of them giggling.

I didn't say anything until she and I walked back to the car, which stood out from the rest in the parking lot by being at least a decade older and three times louder when the engine finally kicked over. When Heather once mentioned needing a new car, Dad had cut her off, "You know what makes a car *really* quiet? Not having one!

Don't be so ungrateful, *you two*," including me for literally no reason whatsoever.

Heather always told Mom and Dad that all her money went toward textbooks and tuition; that's how she explained needing to work so many hours. But in one of those moments that made us more like friends than siblings, she let me in on the truth, which was that she was saving up for a new car. She confessed that she sometimes didn't go to class because of how people would look at her stepping out of her rust-colored Omni. I understood her embarrassment; I felt like that every day.

"So what's his name?" I asked.

"Who?"

"That guy you work with. Your boyfriend."

"My *what?*" she said, laughing.

I felt bad for asking because I'd disrupted her Wallflowers CD, the one she always listened to on repeat in the car. But I liked when we talked as friends.

She said, "You know, before I told him you were my brother, he was going to call security on you. He said you looked like you stole something."

"What did you say?"

"That's the way you always look."

"Dumbass white boys," I said.

I meant it as a joke, but before I could make that clear, Heather slapped me across the chest—Ric Flair style. "Don't say that about him. You sound like Dad."

"Heather, I was just joking."

It took her a few moments to speak again. "Next time, find your own way to the mall. I'm not driving you, anymore."

"I'm really sorry, Heather. Come on. I thought we were talking."

"It wasn't funny," Heather said, "And no, you're not."

"I am, though!"

When we got home I watched the news for any updates on Dominic. I was interested in the story because it was the first time that someone I knew, someone my age, had entered the news cycle. The only people on the news otherwise were grown-ups, which made it easier to pin all the faults of the world on them.

I really miss being able to do that.

There was a car accident on 490 between Penfield and Rochester. And somewhere else, in a suburb of Rochester, fire fighters hosed down a burning car. There were injury updates on Bills' players who were questionable for Sunday's game—thankfully, not Flutie, who had us believing in magic that season.

There was nothing on Dominic. The world had moved on and was prompting me to do the same. Back then, it was easier to move on because it felt like there was more to move on towards.

*

Now in 2020, I don't know.

I'll wake up tomorrow to Andrew Cuomo's daily press conference. He'll remind us of the date, how many of us are sick and in the hospital, and using a line graph, he'll help us imagine how many of us will get sick soon.

On the floor between me and the television, my son plays with his new Legos. He builds a hospital, using an MTA bus toy as an ambulance, "big enough for *everyone*," he says.

4 Aloof

ON THE MORNING of the SATs, I woke up early to cram. I focused on vocabulary words. I already knew I was going to major in English at college—really more for the kind of girls I imagined meeting in English classes. I thought of all the stories I could write, which spared me from having to write them.

I was disrupted by Dad, who shouted up to me that Mom was in the car waiting.

Dad and I hadn't been able to have a conversation since I was in middle school—about the time I started to become the type of kid he didn't know how to deal with. *Insular. Awkward.* More into poetry and music than sports. Dad seemed to take the fact that I couldn't talk to him about sports as an excuse not to talk to me about anything. Including growing up in Guam, which was where most of our family still lived. But because he didn't tell me about Guam, it became this abstract place. Like all the other places in the world I wanted to visit: the cities in Europe I learned about in Global Studies; New York City, outside of MTV Studios. Whenever I asked about growing up in Guam, Dad would reply, "What's so bad about *here?*"—so soon I just stopped asking.

I already had my shirt picked out for Nicole's party—James advised me against the Smashing Pumpkins shirt I got at Hot Topic because in his words "no one likes them," so I chose a buttoned-down shirt from Structure that would help me look like everyone else. James and I had made plans to meet up at his place beforehand. He was really excited to show me how good of a driver he was becoming.

"Are you nervous?" Mom asked me as we headed to the SAT test site.

I was thinking about Nicole's party, so it took me a second to realize she was referring to the test.

"Maybe a little."

"I know you will be fine. You'll figure it out. You always do. You're a smart boy."

It was Mom's first day off in two weeks. She was already dressed for my birthday lunch, after the test, with Papa and Grandma. She had even put in her contacts, which typically meant that she wanted to give herself the option of wearing her sunglasses, purchased at Ames for fifteen bucks. "They were a steal," she'd bragged to me and James, our pockets full of actual steals like Blur's *13*, which I'd grabbed because I liked the song "Tender." It was my comeuppance that I only liked two or three other songs when I heard the whole album.

I was happy Mom was driving me instead of Dad, but there were drawbacks. One was that during the entire ride she kept interrupting my daydreams to tell me how proud she was, changing her words just enough to be funny.

"Just promise me you won't forget about your mother when you leave for college," she chuckled.

"Why do you say stuff like that?" I snapped. I hated how she could make me feel as if wanting to go away for college meant I wanted to forget about them. *Why did I always have to ease their insecurities when they seemed to leave me to figure mine out on my own?* "What makes you think I could forget you?" I said.

*

I forgot so much of the exam, even as I was completing it. I raced through the few questions that had obvious answers. And I skipped over the many questions that confused me—advice from my SAT prep instructor that I only retained because Megan reiterated it. I spent too much time looking around the room at the other students, heads down, their pencils drawing shapes and writing out formulas long committed to memory. I kept wondering, who among us will be the first to die?

Behind the SAT test proctors at the front of the Gymnasium was a small whiteboard, which indicated the amount of time left: TWO ½ HOURS. All I could focus on was why they had written out the number "two" but indicated the half numerically.

Afterward, Mom kept asking about the test. All I could say was that I thought it went well. We avoided the main roads and drove the roads behind the stores that comprised the downtown shopping centers. We passed delivery trucks, loading platforms, and dumpsters. On the delivery trucks were license plates from New Jersey, Vermont, Illinois, and even Oregon. There was graffiti on some of the back walls. Mom commented about it being done by some out-of-town kids. "I've heard it from friends," she explained, "that these kids come here to do stuff like that."

I knew who it really was because I'd heard them bragging about it in the school hallways. "It's kids from my school, Mom."

"Why would they do that to their own town? You go to school with good kids, Cody. That's why we live here."

We spotted Papa's and Grandma's car in the parking lot of the seafood restaurant. Inside they sat alone at opposite ends of a long table, guarded as if someone might try to take one of the other seats between them. Grandma, with her turquoise earrings and matching blouse, spotted us right away and waved. She gestured to Papa to turn around and look, but he remained as he was. Maybe his hearing aid was off. Maybe he just wanted to pester her. He dressed the same way whenever he wasn't on the farm: a light-colored short-sleeve button-down, his chest pocket bulging with a pack of Monarchs. He wore his trucker's hat high on his head, which added a couple of inches to his 5'4" frame. His hands, which were like bricks, rested by the silverware that he'd just wiped clean with his handkerchief.

I gave each of them a quick hug. I'd stopped being too affectionate with them in public sometime in middle school—not that it stopped Grandma from hanging on a second or so longer, or

Papa from holding me in place with a single hand, just because he could.

Heather was all smiles and hugs when she got there. I didn't think she forgave me. She was probably just playing nice while Grandma and Papa were around, because that's what we were told to do.

Even though it was my own birthday lunch, I was mostly quiet during the meal. A part of this was my fault. When I was asked about the SATs, I said that I thought it went fine. There wasn't much else to say, although someone like James could have probably stretched it out a little more. But the rest of it was beyond my control: more than a few of the conversation topics were about family members I didn't know. Uncles and aunts. Cousins roaming the Rockies or the West Coast. Even Heather spoke up every so often, remembering people I'd never heard of. I started to wonder if my family got together without me. I wouldn't have blamed them if they did.

I didn't think any of them would notice if I stepped out, but I announced it anyway. I said it was for fresh air, but it was really just to give myself a break from worrying that I was being too quiet. I took a seat on top of one of the picnic tables on the side of the restaurant. Now early November, all of them were covered with scattered leaves or abandoned candy wrappers from Halloween. We had a couple more weeks until the first snowfall, which was always such an event. I'd chosen the second table from the entrance, simply because it was the cleanest. When a worker pushed through the backdoor from the kitchen, some indecipherable yelling inside followed him out.

Then the door slammed behind him.

The worker stopped a few feet away.

We looked off into the same distance.

We stared up at the homes on the hills that looked down on all of us.

"You wouldn't happen to have a cigarette, would you?" he said.

He wore an Alice in Chains t-shirt under his apron and his face was covered with sweat and smudged with cooking grease. He didn't look mean or tough (as my Dad liked to warn me about people who might come up to me in the world) just overworked. In that second I made the calculation that if we fought, I could take him. I was basing this on literally no evidence whatsoever, aside from my hours of watching *Monday Night Raw*.

"Sorry, I don't smoke." I meant it when I apologized, because sharing a smoke with a complete stranger seemed like a cool thing to do.

When I returned inside, Dad loudly asked if I'd been taking a dump. "You look lighter, dude," he snickered.

The birthday cake appeared immediately after I sat. It was a vanilla cake, which Mom had in her mind was my favorite because I said so when I was in Kindergarten. A few waiters joined in as my family sang "Happy Birthday." Even some of the other customers, who had looked over at me after Dad's joke, started singing. I finally smiled once the singing stopped, and this was the moment Mom captured on camera. I didn't even realize a picture had been taken until I heard Mom dialing the disposable camera for another picture.

*

Mom had that picture of us on the wall behind her during our last FaceTime. Next to it, a picture of Papa and Grandma seated side-by-side on the back of someone's pickup truck—sometime in the '80s. And next to that, a picture of Heather and her husband. Above all of us, a picture of my son, their only grandchild—as Mom loved pointing out.

*

"Do you have any fun plans tonight for your birthday?" Grandma asked as they were getting ready to leave the restaurant.

"I have a friend's party," I answered, low enough so no one else could hear.

I talked more with Grandma than I did with anyone else in the family. She was the only one who knew about my notebook of poems. And she was the only one who knew about all the colleges I planned on applying to.

"I don't know why you think you need to go so far," she'd once said. "You can belong here. With us."

I thought she was saying that because that was what grandmas said. I didn't realize until years later that she was right.

Later when I stepped out, I said I was going to spend the night at James's. He was waiting in the lot for me in his neighbor's car, which was more rust than vehicle and was missing the gas cover. The back window on the driver's side had been replaced by a clear garbage bag taped to the frame, and a taillight was shattered. The license plates were from Georgia.

I tapped on the driver's-side window because James was pretending he didn't see me. I thought he was going to make me hit the window with my fist before he let me in.

"Ready to meet some bitches, birthday boy?"

"What?"

"Just kidding. Get in."

The car squealed when James put it in reverse, and we looked at each other, smiling nervously, not sure what the sound meant. To our relief, the sound stopped when he put the car in drive.

"So how was your lunch with your family?"

"Heather's still not talking to me."

"Do they all think you're weird for not wanting to hang out with your friends on your birthday?"

"I am though," I said, and I blew him a kiss.

We'd passed the McDonald's when James asked if I'd heard the latest about Dominic. "I heard that his parents sent him to live with his grandparents in Pennsylvania."

"Can you leave the state if you have charges pending against you?"

James shrugged. "Honestly, I think people are making stuff up at this point. I was just sharing because I thought you wanted to hear."

James was using different feet for the gas and brake pedals. I hadn't done much driving since Dad kept calling me stupid when he tried to teach me, but I at least knew that you were supposed to use the same foot for both pedals. I was about to correct him when James asked about the SATs.

"I think I did all right."

"Man, you suck at small talk! Good thing I do all the talking for us."

"I can talk for myself."

"Yeah, like *when*?"

Giving specific instances would make it seem like I'd had a response ready. It was better to let it go, although it did bother me.

*

The front of Nicole's house looked like a dealership: new, or new-ish, cars were parked in rows on the lawn, more lined the driveway, and a few were on the side of the road. I thought about how these kids' parents bought these cars only for their kids to drive home drunk in them. Her house was in the middle of the lot: it was one-story tall, with yellow siding on the top and lime-green siding on the bottom. There was a barn in the back with most of its roof missing. In the front yard, a ten-year-old Geo Prizm was on cinderblocks, for sale at $500.

We entered the house without knocking after seeing other people do the same. Inside, everyone was walking around without a care. From room to room, from inside to outside and back again, wherever they wanted. Everyone was holding red Solo cups, which I'd never seen before and thought Nicole might have had specially made for her party.

"Should we get one?" I asked, and James teased, "What, you think they're souvenir cups or something? Like at Disney World."

"Like either of us have been to Disney World, dude."

We followed people to the backyard to the keg. It looked like a metal barrel floating in a tub of water, like something that belonged in an automobile. I paid close attention to how James angled the tap when he poured his drink, so I could recreate it. I stopped pouring my cup halfway because I was failing so badly.

Nicole smiled when she saw us. She threw her arms around my neck in a "hello." She smelled like one of those perfume counters at Macy's, a mixture of strawberries and sun. She turned to some of her classmates nearby and introduced us. "Cody is one of my friends from work. It was his birthday this week. You guys want to sing to him?"

She led them in a rendition of "Happy Birthday" that was a bit out of sync, a bit out of tune, but was way better than the rendition I'd gotten in Gym class from Brian and his friends. I thanked them, these complete strangers, and meant it.

There were enough people in the backyard to fill an entire auditorium. "Damn, girl, you got a lot of friends," James said.

Nicole looked around and just shrugged. "I go to school with most of them. You know how word spreads."

"Is anyone from work coming?" I asked.

"Erin is here," she answered. "She's probably with her new boyfriend."

"And where's *your* boyfriend, Nicole?" said James.

Nicole pulled me close. "He's right here."

Joke or not, it was the first time someone ever thought to refer to me as their boyfriend. I was smiling without realizing it. James looked like he was about to crack a joke, but he ended up not. We were about to head back inside when they noticed my half-filled cup.

"Top yourself off," Nicole said.

My pour, to Nicole's and James's amusement, was all foam. Nicole tried coaching me about how to angle my cup, but I never got it right. When we were almost to the door, Nicole broke away to talk to a group of girls.

We got inside but had no one to talk to. Both of us just looked around and waited for someone to say something to us. As confident as James could be sometimes, he looked just as awkward as I did at that moment. Eventually we found ourselves huddled in the back corner of the kitchen, not far from the microwave, which two guys were using to heat up gas-station burritos. One of them was playing drums on the top of it, while the other shouted the chorus of the song playing.

I accidentally made eye contact with the singer, and he said to me, "These guys are my favorite."

I just nodded in response. I couldn't even hear who was playing.

"I could tell you liked it," he went on; he looked like Kurt Cobain with dark hair and had the pointiest chin I'd ever seen. "You look like you listen to 311."

"Totally," his friend added, "You look like the little Mexican guy that raps."

"No, I don't."

"You kind of do though!"

"No, he *really* doesn't," James said to back me up.

"Do you think all brown people look the same?" I added.

They slinked off with their burritos. Their food made the whole kitchen smell like a fart, so we moved back outside before we could be blamed.

Outside was more crowded than before. I wondered where everyone was coming from. Some emerged from the woods in the back. Others were coming from the barn that I assumed was off-limits. Close to us, two boys started wrestling. One dropped to a knee and shot in for a takedown, and the other partially blocked it, and they scrambled for dominance in the dirt. People who knew them gathered around and cheered them on. I hoped that the match stayed a stalemate because I was already starting to feel bad for whoever lost.

I was still sipping my beer, but James had finished his, so we inched back to the keg, which is where someone grabbed me from behind and started shaking me by the shoulders. They spun me around—it was Ben, from my job that used to be *our* job. He was sweating from every pore in his face. His hair was gelled flat on the sides and back and spiked on top. His cheeks, always rosy, looked more flushed than usual.

"How are you?" I asked.

I probably would have hugged him if he wasn't so sweaty.

"Great," Ben seemed to slur, smiling big. "I'm *so* great right now."

I struggled to follow Ben's line of thought as he went on about studying for the SATs, his classes at school, the song playing, another song he'd heard earlier, a movie he'd rented, and girls at the party he was going to try to hook up with.

"Any 'Pickles'?" I asked.

Ben furrowed his brow.

"Pickles," I repeated, "Remember, from work?"

"I'm trying to forget," he said. And suddenly, he pointed past us and screamed, "Erin!" He flung his arm around her shoulder when she came over. She was dressed in a black Aéropostale polo and flared jeans. Her mid-riff was showing, and all of us took turns trying not to stare. "Hey, Erin, do you have any weed? I don't know who to ask."

Erin shrugged him off but made sure to do it smiling. Ben turned to me, his eyes sharp. "Why aren't you drinking?"

"He is," James replied, handing me a cup with no foam. "He just holds it better than some people."

Ben leaned close to Erin and almost lost his footing. "This is such a great time," he shouted. "And look at this guy," pointing to me, "drinking and still so serious. Hey, chug that beer, man. Chug! Chug! Chug!"

Erin pointed toward the house. "Ben, some girl inside was looking for you. You should go find her."

He rushed off, all of us watching him for the spectacle he was making of himself.

"How long's he been here?" I asked.

"Not long. An hour, maybe."

"Maybe he was drinking beforehand," I said. I wanted to help Ben save face, however annoying he was being at the moment. I still felt like I owed him for sitting with me when no one else would.

"I think some people just get really excited about going to parties, especially when it's their first one. You okay, Cody?"

"Cody's fine," James answered.

"Yeah, I'm fine," I stated, if only to prove that I didn't need James talking for me.

"So where's this boyfriend of yours?" James asked. "Shouldn't he be protecting you from dorks like Ben?"

"He's inside," she answered, catching herself afterward, "So Nicole told you? She keeps telling everyone he's my boyfriend. We just like to hang out, is all."

"That's all?" James pressed.

Erin was visibly uncomfortable, but she knew enough to hide it with a smile. "Nicole just likes to talk about me as if I can't talk for myself."

"I hate it when friends do that," I said.

"But she means well," Erin replied, just as James slapped my arm and said, "Hey, fuck you, man."

Ben was barreling towards us again. Each of us braced ourselves for having to deal with him, so it was a relief when we saw Jay beside him. Erin must have slipped away at the first sight of Ben returning. She was gone when we turned to look for her.

"Here he is!" Ben said to Jay, "Still nursing that same beer!"

Jay was in his work clothes, his shirt unbuttoned to show off the tribal sun tattoo on his left pec. It was all anyone could talk about at work when he first got it. Jay had bragged about getting it cheap in a friend's basement.

"What's up, Player B?" Jay said.

"What's up, Jay?" I said, knowing at this point I could do nothing about the "Player B" nickname. "I thought you were working."

"This guy," Jay said to Ben and James, "You writing a book?"

I started to reply, but Jay held up his hands in mock surrender. "Relax. I'm messing with you." He looked at Ben and wrapped his arm around his shoulder, "Happy to see my dude Ben though! Work really sucks without you."

Ben smiled and returned the half-hug, "I miss you too, Jay."

Jay shrugged him off when he hung on for too long. "You guys see Erin's boyfriend? I want to take a look at him. I heard he's going to swim for Penn State."

"I have P.E. with him," Ben said. "He's an asshole."

Jay smiled. "All guys are assholes. Some are just more honest about it." He then glanced at his watch and said he had to get going. "Maybe I'll stop by later," he said, as if we were begging him to return.

Soon after Jay left, Ben sprinted into the woods, his hand pressed over his mouth. We followed him to make sure he was okay and when we finally caught up to him he was on all fours, vomit splashing the ground in front of him.

"You okay?" I asked.

Ben couldn't tell me what a stupid question that was, but James let me know with a look.

"We should probably get him home," James said. "Do you know where he lives?"

"Maybe Nicole or Erin do. I can ask."

I got back to the house as everyone was leaving. Nicole was holding the front door for people, seeing them out.

"What's going on?" I asked.

"My neighbor threatened to call the cops if we didn't stop the party," she answered. "He said people were pissing on his property, which I know isn't true. I told everyone not to go near the barn."

I told her about Ben, and she rolled her eyes. "Well, I'm happy he enjoyed himself because I'm never inviting him again. All he did was grope a couple of my friends and cut people in line at the keg."

She told me Ben's address—she knew it from when they had to do a school project together—and after grabbing a trash bag from the kitchen she followed me to where James was waiting with Ben.

"Are both of you going? I was hoping one of you could help me pick up."

I volunteered right away, and she told me to meet her in the backyard. First, I helped James hoist Ben into the backseat of Will's car. Ben could barely speak, but he farted in thanks.

"You're welcome," I said, and no one laughed.

I gave James the directions that Nicole had given to me.

"You were so quick to stay back with Nicole. Better do something with it," he said, slamming the door shut.

I made my way back to Nicole. Brian and his girlfriend passed me going the opposite direction. He knocked into my shoulder and gave no acknowledgement.

I took the shoulder bump and kept walking.

I heard Dad telling me I needed to stand up for myself.

I heard James calling me "pussy."

Then I heard Nicole. "Over here!"

I spotted her a little ways into the woods, staring down at something.

"Would you like to do the honors?" she said when I got to her.

I followed her eyes to a used condom on the ground. "Where's the wrapper?" I said.

"I don't know. I haven't had time to conduct a full investigation."

"I was thinking we could use the wrapper to pick it up."

"Oh. Smart."

We didn't find the wrapper, so she grabbed some leaves nearby. We walked a little further into the woods to pick up beer cans. Nicole did the picking up. I held the trash bag. The woods were surprisingly clean: a few cans here and there, some cigarette butts.

"You have considerate friends," I said, "Looks like someone cleaned up already."

"The inside is pretty clean too," Nicole said, "I told everyone to throw their trash away because it took me almost all night to pick up after my last party. No one stuck around to help either, so I really appreciate you staying back."

Nicole retrieved an open can of beer and tipped it out. She tossed it towards the trash bag I was holding. I had to move it to the left for the can to go in. Beer splattered my hands and arms, but I ignored it because I wanted her to think it was a clean shot.

"There's a clearing up ahead. We'll check there and then head back. When I was little, my friends and I would go to this spot and pretend to be witches. Then, when *The Craft* came out, oh my God, that was *it* for us," she laughed. "*Light as a feather, stiff as a board. Light as a feather, stiff as a board.*"

I followed her in the dark, my eyes fixed on her feet so I knew where to step. The clearing that Nicole referred to looked like an abandoned campsite. There was a small circle of stones in the middle of it, presumably for a campfire, and the small pieces of trash all over the area reminded me of camping trips with my family and James at Six Flags. This past year we'd been joined by one of my parents' coworkers who had a daughter our age. Who James and I stared at the entire weekend.

We started out on opposite ends of the clearing, picking up beer cans and cigarette butts, as well as some red plastic cups that looked too dirty and beat-up to be from tonight. We met up in the center, and I bent over and picked up what I thought was a joint.

"Looks like your childhood hangout has become a spot for drugs," I said, imitating the drawl of Mr. Mackey on *South Park*.

"That's not a joint." Nicole smiled. "That's a cigarette that someone rolled." Nicole tried to light it a few times before tossing it.

"Is this what you do out here now that you're too old to pretend to be a witch?"

"I *am* a witch," she answered. "And that's not all I do out here, as I'm sure you know." She tossed more trash in my direction. "Jay told me that you've been telling everyone at work that I blow guys from work."

Before I could protest, she continued, "Listen, I'm not stupid. I know that's why some guys like me. It's not because they think I'm pretty or interesting. It's because they think I'll blow them, isn't it?" She looked at me but not for confirmation or rebuttal. Maybe just to see if I was listening. She shook her head. "You're all so predictable."

"*I'm* not like that."

"Maybe you've just never had the chance to be."

She headed back to her house, and I followed. But not too close because I wanted to give her space. I wondered why Jay chose *me* as the person spreading the story.

"I know people gossip about me," she eventually said. "I have nothing to be ashamed about, but I just wish people would mind their own business."

"You know no one knows how to shut up," I said.

And this made her laugh, so I started laughing, too.

"So do you want to hear about it?" she said.

"About what?"

"All those guys I blow."

I stammered, "What? No. That's not any of my... No."

"So, do you want to have sex?" She looked at me without blinking.

I tried not to squirm or look uncomfortable, but that was getting more difficult the longer she stared.

I turned away and started walking back. She put her hand on my shoulder and turned me around. She held my face between her hands so all I could see was her. And her lips. I was so close that I could count the eleven freckles on her nose and see the moon in her eyes.

She released my face and stepped back, laughing. "You're hopeless! How can you be so smart and so dumb?"

"Because I'm not that smart."

"I'm realizing that!"

I took one step closer, then another, until I was standing right against her. We kissed, close-mouthed at first, then I felt her run her tongue across my teeth. It was such a new sensation that I pulled away. Not much—but just enough for her to notice.

We didn't speak the rest of the way back. Every so often Nicole looked back at me, as if waiting for me to say something, but I couldn't think straight.

Nicole went into her house. I didn't follow her, and I wouldn't have known what to do if I did.

James's car was rolling up the driveway. I jogged over to it and hopped inside, even before he could come to a complete stop.

"Where's Nicole?" he asked.

"Sleeping," I replied, buckling up.

We didn't know where to go next. Everyone else from the party had moved on without us, so we headed to Denny's. My stomach felt a little off from the beer, so I didn't really want to eat but James did and he was my ride, so that settled it.

"What was up with that comment you made to Erin?" James said, once we got a table.

"What was up with that comment you made to me in the car? About you always having to talk for me?"

"It's true, isn't it?" James asked.

We sat in silence for a few moments before James continued, "Look. I'm sorry. I didn't mean anything by it."

"I'm sorry too."

"I left Ben on his porch," James said. "I didn't want to knock because all the lights were off, and I didn't feel comfortable carrying him into his house. He was out cold. Figured I'd tell you because I know you guys got along real well."

"Can I tell you something?" I said, before admitting what had happened with Nicole. James's face was all smiles by the end of it, I thought because of how I messed it up.

"Let me guess; you got feelings for her now?" James smirked.

I wasn't sure what feelings I had for her—aside from the ones I'd always had.

"You know the story with her and that co-worker of yours," James went on, "I'm just saying, a girl with that kind of story out there about her, you can't date that girl. Wherever you go with her, all the guys are going to make fun of you."

"I wouldn't care. I could handle it."

James gave me a look, "You hide out in your room for a week whenever someone makes a joke about you. I'm just saying, Nicole's cool, but you don't want to date that kind of girl your first time out."

"What kind of girl is she?"

"You need me to say it?"

5 Constancy

THE RUMOR GOING AROUND school on Monday was that Dominic Hopkins killed himself. It was easy to joke about death when it only seemed to affect other people. But Dominic wasn't other to us.

"*Why they always gotta kill the dark kid?*" James said. I could feel his pain.

But Andrew, who always hated it when James talked "ghetto," tried to change the subject, uncomfortable. "How'd the SATs go, Cody? I was going to call you but I couldn't find your number."

We'd exchanged numbers back in seventh grade when we were paired for a science project. He never called me; I called him. What really stuck with me though was Andrew's disappointment that we were put together. That entire year he'd been trying to buddy up to a group of pale skater kids sitting in the back of the room, sometimes joining them when they made fun of me for my high test scores. Andrew sometimes hid his own scores because they were higher than mine. Lately, he'd started smelling like those kids—that same blend of pharmacy cologne and weed that they wanted the rest of us to find edgy. I was just about to ask him who he was smoking with these days, but I was smart enough to figure it out. He'd used his low score on our last practice test as an opportunity to get Megan to tutor him. That's why Eric was upset, but only because he didn't think of it first.

"I feel pretty good about the SATs. But we'll see," I said.

"All of Saturday was great for Cody," James cut in. "Quick. Tell him what happened with Nicole."

My face flushed right away, and Andrew smiled smugly at my embarrassment.

"Who?" he said.

I told him, and he just shook his head.

"I don't know her," he said, and that was enough for him, because now he was ready to return to our previous conversation about Dominic, on his terms. "I don't know if Dominic killing himself is true, but I think I'm going to use it for a story I'm writing for English class. It's about a straight-A student who is also a star athlete getting busted for drugs right before graduation, costing him the college he wants to go to."

"Ooh, what college is that? Geneseo? Buffalo?" James scoffed. "Maybe some place exotic like... Albany?"

"Stanford," Andrew answered.

"Boring," James said.

"Stanford is a good college. It's *my* first choice. A lot of famous writers teach there."

"What makes you think you can write about a brown kid?" James said.

"Who says my main character is a minority? He's white."

James turned to me, purposefully excluding Andrew just to piss him off. "They want to take our stories, even when we mess up. *Sheeee-iiiiiit*."

"Why do you talk like that, James?" Andrew snapped. "You grew up in the same town as the rest of us. Stop sounding stupid."

"He's joking," I said. I meant it as an explanation, but it sounded too much like I was apologizing on James's behalf.

The bell rang, and we dispersed for class. As Andrew headed down a different hallway than the rest of us, James shouted after him, "Keep writing your dumbass stories that no one will ever read, Andrew."

"You don't have to be like that," I said.

"Why not? That guy is the worst. *Stanford. Stanford. Stanford.* He thinks he's so smart, and he's probably going to just up end at SUNY Bumblefuck like everyone else."

"Thanks, man," I said.

"Not you, dude!"

Constancy

*

For the rest of the day, the rumors about Dominic Hopkins heightened in severity and gruesomeness. Everyone was less concerned with the truth and more concerned with one-upping each other. When one girl in Pre-Calc told some boys that they shouldn't laugh about suicide, they gleefully told her to kill herself.

It wasn't until Gym class that Dominic's name stopped being mentioned, and that was because of Brian. Brian made it clear that he didn't want to hear any more gossip about Dominic. Then he turned to me. "Hey, Taitano!" again mispronouncing it, "do anything for your birthday?"

His transgression of social protocol caught everyone's attention. Brian's whole group of friends did not seem to know what to do—including Pete off to the side of them, a moon in their orbit.

"Just hung out," I answered.

Brian sized me up for a few seconds, then asked me what he probably wanted to ask in the first place. "Did I see you at Nicole Bradshaw's party?"

"I was there, but I don't remember seeing you."

"I wasn't sure it was you," Brian said, quickly adding, "Not that I thought you were someone else. Just that . . . I don't know . . . you being there didn't add up. I've known Nicole since middle school. She used to date one of my friends."

Dominic's name passed between us unsaid. I didn't know that Nicole and Dominic had dated, but it didn't matter to me.

Brian's lips curled in a knowing smile. "She can be a bit . . . *mouthy* though, right?"

It took me too long to realize what Brian could mean by this.

"Pretty cool not to have to kiss your own hand for once, huh?" said Pete, laughing right away at his own joke.

"Man, shut up. Have you ever even been on a date?" Brian snapped.

"Your mom doesn't count," someone from the group added.

"Pete's mom kissed *this*," Brian said and gestured to his crotch.

I remembered Pete's mom from a field trip to the Planetarium in fifth grade. Her housewife haircut, dyed golden blonde, and her unseasonably deep tan. She smelled like cherry Chapstick and fabric softener.

"Good thing she keeps her lips moisturized," I added.

"I remember that!" Brian said. When he started laughing his friends immediately joined in. "She used to put Chapstick on every five seconds!" As Brian and his friends continued talking about Pete's mom, his eyes darkened and went blank.

I walked away before I had to contribute another comment, but I looked back one last time at that abyss in Pete's eyes. I would recognize this same look years later after college when I saw Pete sitting alone at a bar. I'd gone out that night with James, who I quickly lost, and wandered around downtown Canandaigua for other people I might recognize. All I saw was Pete, and that look in his eyes, and I left; no regrets.

*

But I regretted right away not speaking up for Nicole—especially after what she'd said in the woods. Maybe she was right about me being like other guys. I had my chance to prove her wrong and botched it. I needed to speak to her, to make it right before she heard.

I wasn't strong enough to go alone, so I stopped at James's after school to get him to bike with me.

"What do you got to say to her?" James asked.

"I want to say sorry."

"Man, for what?"

I couldn't answer exactly. This, despite all the SAT words I had learned.

James gave me a few more seconds to respond then shrugged. "Okay, dude, whatever," and we hopped on our bikes.

6 Reprisal

WE ARRIVED AT THE HEIGHT of the dinner rush. Customers were usually such a bother and a bore, but they were doing me two favors at that moment. They gave me enough time to formulate what I was going to say to Nicole, and they blocked the Employee-of-the-Month plaque with Jay's stupid name on it.

Erin and Nicole were at the registers, and Robbie was behind them in the grill area with a few of the daytime crew sticking around for overtime pay. Todd, sweat lining his head where his hairline would be if he had one, scurried from the fries to the drive-thru window, assembling and handing out orders.

James went in Erin's line. He waved and smiled big when she saw him, and she rolled her eyes. I went to Nicole's line. Unfortunately this meant that in addition to having to talk to Nicole by myself, I would get to the front of the line first. Nicole was always a little faster than Erin, who would often pause and stare at the screen in between customers. I knew this because she told me.

I moved slowly toward the front counter, Nicole watching me.

"You come here a lot when you don't work, don't you?" she said, when I finally reached her.

I muttered something—part laugh, part "*yeah*" or "*maybe*," totally indistinguishable and not-quite English. "When's your break?"

Next to me James stepped up to the counter and immediately started ordering and changing everything he'd just ordered. He was giving me more time with Nicole. "Ooh, that sounds good. Wait, let me get that instead. That come with onions? Okay, I want it without." The entire time, Erin's eyes were on him like lasers. "*Hold up, girl,* what's on the Big 'N' Tasty? *How big we talking?* Does size matter to you?"

"Cody!" shouted Todd from the drive-thru. "It's dinner rush. Flirt with Nicole some other time."

"Shut up, Todd! He's thinking about his order," Nicole shouted. Then to me, "Give me ten or fifteen minutes."

James and I headed outside and shared his order of twenty nuggets. Cars swerved passed us on their way to the drive-thru. Other cars sped into parking spots on the far side of the lot.

A red pickup truck plastered with bumper stickers pulled into the furthest row of spots. Two men a little older than us stepped out, their eyes empty of everything except anger. They wore matching hats, rims overly bent into the shape of an omega sign. They whispered to each other and nodded at us as they approached. "What are you little shits lookin' at?" they snapped. We were smart enough to pretend not to hear them as they pushed through the door.

A minute or so later they walked back out, their laughter loud and defiant. We just assumed they were still laughing at us. We looked down at the outdoor table we were sitting at and waited for the men to pass.

Nicole and Erin joined us. Erin was clutching a small brown bag of food already seeping grease at the bottom.

Across the lot the guys were joined by a couple more.

"We got some nuggets left over, if either of you want," I said.

Without acknowledging me, Nicole and Erin helped themselves. Erin placed the brown bag on the bench beside her.

"Thanks," Nicole whispered, "we were starving."

"Cody, you're not going to run your mouth about us, anymore, are you?" Erin sighed.

Nicole shoved her arm.

Erin looked apologetic for a second, just a second, before she started laughing.

"What's so funny?" James said.

"Ask Cody. He likes to talk so much."

"Erin," Nicole said, firmer this time, "shut up."

The men by the pickup truck yipped and howled.

James and I suddenly realized who they'd actually been laughing at as they left the restaurant. We were so used to people being racist that we still had to learn all the other ways people could be shitty.

Nicole nodded toward them. "One of those pricks groped me while he was ordering. He put his hand up to my face and touched my cheek. And when I told him not to do that, he grabbed my chest."

"Why didn't you pull away?" James asked.

"It's not that easy," she answered. "I was about to say something, but he just walked off."

James looked confused. "I don't know, Nicole. It seems. . ."

"I'm really sorry, Nicole," I said, interrupting James, "What did Todd do?"

"He was too busy yelling at Robbie for messing up a drive-thru order. It wasn't Robbie's fault, though. Todd accidentally put 10 hamburgers instead of 1, and before he corrected it, Robbie had already made everything."

"Their mistake is our gain though," Erin interjected, waving her arm over the food she'd just dumped out of the brown bag onto the table. "Bon Appetit, boys."

"I'm impressed Robbie got all this out so fast," I said.

"He's gotten really good, actually," Nicole explained. "Todd's just a prick."

"He's like that to all of us."

"Yeah, but . . . it's been worse since the day my car died and Todd kept trying to drive me home. I got a ride with Robbie instead."

I must have tensed up somehow. Or made a face. Or done something else without realizing, because Nicole continued, "Relax, he just drove me home. We smoked a bowl in my driveway and that was it. I've only made out with one guy lately—*you*."

I looked at everyone around the table. It was Erin who finally broke the silence, "Yep, we all know, stud."

A black Accord swung into the parking lot and pulled up to

the group of men by the pickup truck. They hopped inside the Accord, and the car peeled out. One of them blew kisses at us.

I looked over at the pickup that they'd left unguarded. Its paint was so red it looked like it was shining, even in the autumn dusk. Definitely too pretty and new to be left unattended.

Their mistake. Our gain.

I grabbed one of the hamburgers that Erin had dumped onto our table, unwrapping it while running across the parking lot, and threw it into the side of the truck. The hamburger exploded on impact. The meat bounced off the side and fell limply on the ground. Ketchup and mustard streaked and spotted. One sad pickle clung to the car until it too fell. When I got back to the table, everyone looked at me stunned.

James then grabbed another one of the hamburgers and ran towards the pickup. And Erin grabbed the rest of the food, stuffed it into the bag, and chased after him. The two of them unloaded each of the food items onto the vehicle, sometimes even picking up the deconstructed pieces and hurling them a second time.

"I'm sorry Erin was being a bitch just now," Nicole said.

"She's definitely the first person to ever accuse me of talking too much."

"She's my best friend. She's got my back, is all."

"I didn't want to make you mad. I just didn't know what to say. I'm sorry. I'm sorry for a lot."

One final splat of meat and condiments on the pickup, followed by cheers from James and Erin, who high-fived one another.

"I hope they don't get in trouble," Nicole said.

"With who?" I asked. "The cops? Todd?" I couldn't think of anybody who would care enough to do anything about it. "I wonder how I could spin getting arrested as a positive in my college application essay."

"Depends on what college you're going to. Some probably won't care." And I remembered my next meeting with Mr. Greer and what I had to write for him.

Reprisal

Nicole's face was aglow with passing headlights.

This is how I see her even now.

I had no delusions of being anything but a stupid small-town kid, but in that instant she made me feel like I could be more.

"Do you ever think how weird it is that we'll all be somewhere else next year?" I asked.

"Is that what you spend all your time thinking about?"

I shrugged. "Sometimes I think about all the things I missed out on."

"What do you think you missed? You think the rest of us are just out hogging all the fun? Do you think you're the only one waiting for college?"

I wondered if I should admit that I did. "I wasn't really going to Dominic's party that night. Yours was the first party I'd ever been to."

"Aww, I was your first?"

I know I must have blushed. I definitely lost my breath for a second when I went to laugh.

Erin and James were making their way back to us. James kept lagging behind, getting Erin to match his pace, and I could have sworn that he was doing this to give me extra time. I needed to make good on it. I owed it to James. And to myself.

"Do you want to go out sometime?"

Right away, she started laughing. "Wow, I wasn't sure you had it in you. You seemed so distant on Saturday. I kept waiting for you to say something. . . . You know what? Let's do it. But only as friends, okay? I'm not looking to date anyone right now."

I immediately accepted. "It's a ... *date*?"

"Kind of."

We made no concrete plans beyond her picking me up at 7 o'clock on Saturday.

When Erin and Nicole returned to work, James and I biked around downtown and visited the CD sections at Ames and Wal-Mart. We passed McDonald's again on our way back. The two men had returned to their pickup truck by then. We saw them kicking the food away from their truck and trying to wipe the sides of it clean. They kept looking around for someone, anyone, to bear the brunt of their rage.

      We glided by in the dark. We waited until we figured we were out of sight and then burst out laughing. Once we started, we couldn't stop. We laughed the entire ride home.

7 Instigate

THE NEXT DAY was the first day at school since the arrest that no one mentioned Dominic. Back to the usual gossiping circles. The same social divisions on display. High school, where we watched each other every day, but learned nothing about one another.

I found my friends in the school atrium. I wasn't sure what James, Andrew, and Eric had been talking about before I showed up, but whatever it was, it had escalated into another argument between Andrew and James.

"Our country's the richest in the world," Andrew was saying, "If you're struggling here, that says something about *you*, not our society."

"Why you always talk like yours is the only opinion that matters?" James said.

"Listen," Andrew said, "I wrote a whole paper on our country's economics for AP History last year. And you know what I got on it? I got an A. Don't challenge me on this, James. I'll school you."

"Megan was in that class, right?" Eric asked.

We all stopped to look at him. "Damn, dude, you're hard up," James said, which was just about the only thing he and Andrew could ever agree on.

I helped Eric by changing the subject. "You're taking the SATs next weekend, aren't you?"

"This weekend," Eric said.

"I'm tired of talking about the SATs," Andrew said, "I just want them over, so we can all talk about other stuff."

"Like what?" Eric asked. "There's not much else left. We're all leaving for college soon."

Andrew nodded toward James. "Not this guy. He'll be flipping burgers the rest of his life."

"You know something, Andrew—"

But before James could continue, Megan called out to Andrew and distracted all of us.

"That's my sign, boys," Andrew boasted, eyeing Eric in particular, before he took off after her.

"He was telling me they started hanging out on weekends," Eric explained as we dragged our feet to our first period classes. "They smoke weed together, too. *I* don't even know who to *buy* it from. You guys know?"

The first person I thought of was Robbie at work. James probably knew some people too—co-workers at Burger King. Nobody Eric would know because his parents didn't want him working when he should be focusing on the SATs and college applications.

"I just don't get it," Eric said. "What does Megan see in him?"

"Maybe she's got an acne fetish," James said, trying to help. "That's good news! It means you're *too good looking* for her, Eric."

Eric broke off from us to head into his class. I broke off next to meet with Mr. Greer. While I was still within earshot, James shouted to me from down the hall, "Stop by my place after school, I got something to show you," catching looks from everyone, including Mr. Greer, who I could tell was judging me based on my friendships.

My meeting with Mr. Greer was quick—partly because I didn't have anything to show him and partly because he was meeting with a second student right after me, one who just got a sports scholarship to UConn.

"What do you mean, you have nothing?" Mr. Greer said. "You *do* want to help yourself stand out, *don't you?*"

I stayed quiet, rather than admit that standing out was the *last* thing I wanted to do.

In this meeting he pivoted from encouraging me to "write about Guam" to writing about my upbringing and "how difficult it must have been, and how college would be a way for them to help you...."

Instigate

I didn't want to write about my difficulties though. I wanted to write about my friends—even more so after I understood I wouldn't be allowed to.

When I got to James's after school, I understood exactly what he meant when he said he had something to show me. The car! James had bought Will's car. He had a car, which meant we had a car because that's how it was between us.

We thought of all the places we could go. Day trips to Niagara Falls, or down South 81, which I remembered from signs on my way to my grandparents' house. There were thruways in every direction. Roads that could take us anywhere, including to other roads that could take us further. So many possibilities—we just needed to figure out where to start.

We settled on the mall.

"So where're you and Nicole going on your date?" James asked.

"It's not a date," I said. "But I was thinking of going to see a movie." A movie would spare me from the pressure of conversation.

"Why don't you take her to the arcade?" James said.

A lot of our classmates went to the arcade on weekends. The arcade, as well as the bowling alley, was a great way to see people outside of school if that was your thing. James and I had gone there once but left after twenty minutes when the kids wearing Korn shirts and JNCO pants gave us looks like we didn't belong.

As if reading my mind, James added, "Get over it, dude. If we never went to all the places where people acted weird toward us, we'd have nowhere to go!"

*

And here we are now, decades later, all of us, with nowhere to go. In the last week my son and I have built a whole neighborhood with his Lego set—a school, a firehouse, even a McDonald's. He parks his toy car, the one that most resembles our white Subaru, in front of

McDonald's because he wants to go there so badly. To him, our car is magical, taking him anywhere he wishes. Even if we can't go inside when we get there, doors locked, drive-thru only.

*

James's first car was a bit less magical than the last time we'd used it. The glove compartment—bursting with water-stained papers and candy wrappers that once strewn the floors—now hung from one hinge against my knees on the passenger side.

"Nice of Will to clean it up for you," I said.

"He also left these," James said, digging around until a couple of condoms were visible.

All I could think about was Will using those condoms in this car. "Maybe you should scrub the seats."

"Why?" James reached through the opening between the driver and passenger side and ran a hand across the surface of the backseat. "Feels fine to me. Also, check this out," and he reached into his pocket and flaunted his driver's license, recently arrived in the mail.

"Six feet tall, huh?" I smirked.

"Shut up," snatching it back from me, "*I'm taller than you, bitch.*"

We made it to the mall in less than twenty minutes. Every other time I'd gone with Heather or with someone else in my family, it had taken almost half an hour.

"That's because I'm a smooth son-of-a-bitch," James gloated.

We walked in without knowing where to go. We were in no rush. We had money in our pockets and the whole afternoon free.

"I'm going to FYE," I said.

"Okay. I'm going to the food court to look for girls," James replied, walking off.

At FYE I ran into Heather and Jennifer, also wandering the aisles and looking at the various album covers.

"Jennifer, you remember my brother," Heather said. I was about to say "Guten Tag" to be funny, when Heather continued, "What are you doing here, Cody?"

"I got a ride from James. I didn't know you were working today."

"I'm not"—was all she said, before Jennifer interjected—"But I am. I'll see you later, Heather?"

Heather nodded and waved to her friend, and only when Jennifer was gone did she turn toward me. "So, where's James? In the movie section trying to figure out which movies have sex scenes?"

I shook my head and laughed—mostly because it was silly to think that two seventeen-year-old dudes like me and James didn't already know which movies had sex scenes and which ones didn't.

"He's at the food court looking at girls," I said, and realized only afterward how that made James sound.

"Why didn't you join him?" Heather asked.

"I wanted to look at CDs."

Heather scrunched her face. "This store can be so boring though, right? The same CDs. I was actually thinking of going to the food court for coffee. Come on. I'll buy you one."

We got to the food court and found James sitting two tables away from a group of girls. Not even hiding the fact that he was gawking at them.

"Is this all you two do here, gawk?" Heather asked, sitting.

"No," we replied in unison, and we totally sounded defensive.

"Well," James added afterward.

"Well, what?" Heather said.

"Well, I don't got to anymore, now that you're here."

Heather groaned. "I'm going to get coffees for me and Cody. You want anything, James?"

"I want you to go out with me," he said.

Shaking her head, she turned away.

James repeated himself, louder this time, but Heather kept on walking.

"Way to make me look stupid in front of your sister," James said.

"How was I to know that you'd be sitting here staring like a stalker?"

I turned to see how far away Heather was. When I saw she wasn't looking, I stole a quick glance at the table of girls that James had been eyeing.

"Admire from the bleachers, boys," a familiar voice said as he passed by on his way to the girls' table.

Dominic Hopkins looked almost the same as he did when I last saw him after Gym Class. Leaner—not sickly-looking but athletic. He'd also grown a Johnny Depp-style goatee, which was something I couldn't pull off even if I stopped shaving for a year.

Dominic hugged each of the girls in greeting before taking a seat in the middle of them. He sat facing us, and the way he stared right through us made me think *we*, not he, had become *personae non gratae*. But did he ever become *persona non grata?* or just elevated to myth?

He whispered something to get them all to look over. A second later, he had them pointing and laughing.

"Guess he's not dead like everyone at school was saying," James shrugged. "What do you think he just said to those girls?"

"Does it matter?"

Heather joined us with the coffees. "Is there a reason why there's a table full of cute girls laughing at you, and the two of you are staring at the guy?"

"He goes to our school," I said.

When we left it at that, Heather asked, "Did he say something mean to you? You want me to kick his ass?"

James scoffed. "We could do that for ourselves, Heather."

Heather looked at Dominic then back at the two of us. "Maybe if you worked together."

One of the girls kept playfully shoving Dominic, whenever he teased her, which he did often. Eventually, he put his arm around her

Instigate

waist and pulled her against him.

"He a friend of yours?" Heather asked.

"He's that kid that got arrested," James said.

"I heard about that," Heather replied, "I thought Dad said he was a friend of yours."

"Dad said that?"

"Dad says lots of things."

Dominic and his friends left without cleaning up after themselves. Heather had to leave for class, but before she did, she walked over to Dominic's table and pushed in their seats and threw away their garbage.

James and I watched her but didn't offer to help. I resented her for cleaning up after people—and for doing it so publicly. "Just bothers me when people leave a mess," she'd always say.

James and I stuck around for another hour. Eventually we strolled back to the other end of the mall where we'd parked. We looked into each store we passed, imagining ourselves wearing the clothes in the windows. We knew we were more than our passing reflections though. We just had to figure out *what* for ourselves.

8 Neophyte

I WAITED IN THE PARKING LOT in front of my townhouse. It was already 7:09, and Nicole's car was nowhere in sight. Others came and went, each of them tricking my eyes. The night was making every car look like the one car in the world I was waiting for. Finally it swerved around the corner and sped toward me, stopping just short of where I stood.

"You weren't going to move?" Nicole called out her window.

I walked around to the passenger side and hopped in. "I trust you."

"Now why would you do that?"

As we drove to the arcade, I thought of telling her about seeing Dominic at the mall. But it wasn't like anything happened, aside from Dominic embarrassing me and James, and I wasn't completely sure how close Nicole and Dominic were anymore. I wondered how much she had known about Dominic's whereabouts—all while so many kids at my school were gossiping he was dead.

I complimented her taste in music, which I could see (from the scratched CDs scattered on the floor) included Fiona Apple, Radiohead, and Weezer.

The last one in particular made me smile big. "'Butterfly is my favorite song," I said.

"Mine, too," Nicole replied. "But let's keep that secret. It's not one of the cool things to like right now."

"I like this album almost as much as their first."

"That's what everyone says," she replied.

I went to put the CD into the player, but she stopped me by pointing out the cracks and scratches on the disc. "I've been meaning to replace it."

We got to the arcade without hitting a single red light—one of those rare occurrences in a small town that could make you believe in God. We turned into the parking lot, but an Alero cut us off and took the last parking spot. Nicole honked and cursed at them. We circled a couple of times until another spot opened up.

"See? Just got to think positive," Nicole said, forgetting that she'd been cursing at the Alero a minute ago.

As we headed inside, someone called out behind us: "Nicole, what's up?"

Four guys stalked us up the entrance steps. A militia of polo shirts, khaki pants, and puka shell necklaces. They were coming from the same Alero that had cut us off.

"Hi, Kyle," Nicole said, before adding the names of the rest of them as they filed past.

"Who's your friend?" Kyle asked, sizing me up.

"This is Cody," Nicole answered. "We work together."

Kyle leaned back in laughter. "One of your *Mickie D* buddies!"

Nicole rolled her eyes. "Cody, these are some guys from school. Kyle and I are in the same Government class."

"That's all you have to say about me?"

When I shook hands with Kyle, I made sure to tuck my elbow—as Dad instructed me.

"You sure you don't work at Taco Bell, man. I swear, you look more like a Taco Bell guy," Kyle said.

I knew what he was getting at. Like many, he knew how to be racist without being outright racist. He'd learned how to hide behind stupid jokes, but saying something wouldn't have helped me. All I could do was refuse to look away from them—and it took all for me not to.

Bored by my lack of a response, Kyle turned back toward Nicole. "Was that your Civic I cut off just now? I can't believe that thing is still running."

"Not everyone's parents buy them a new car just for being born," she said.

"I pay for gas," Kyle said, adding "sometimes" low enough so only we could hear. "You still got that junker on your front lawn? Man, that thing isn't even worth a full tank of gas."

Nicole rolled her eyes and walked away, grabbing me by the hand so I knew to follow. We headed to the section of video games, while Kyle and his friends lingered by the pool tables.

"Oh, okay, bye, Nicole," Kyle called out. "So long, Taco Bell!"

Without looking back, Nicole flipped them off.

"Are you okay?" I asked, once we stopped at a two-player car-racing game.

We sat there watching the same simulated race play out. The same winding streets and cheering crowds.

"Do you want to go? We can go."

She shook her head, eventually forcing a smile. "We're at an arcade. Let's play something. This should be fun."

I smiled. "Then let's have fun."

We raced a few rounds. Nicole won each time. I tried to keep up, then catch up, before careening into a cliff or building. Before erupting into flames. It was getting harder to laugh it off each time it happened.

"Here, let me help you," she said.

She put her hands over mine and guided me. She told me when and how much to ease my foot off the pedal. She kept telling me to relax.

"Well, thanks anyway for your help," I said, after my final crash. "You're a better driving instructor than my dad."

We walked around the part of the arcade that shielded us from Kyle and the rest of his group. We didn't stop at any particular game, slowing just enough to watch other people play and tease each other when they won.

"Do you want to play anything else?" she asked.

I looked around and shook my head. I glanced over at the pool tables. Kyle and his friends were gone. I half-expected them to creep up behind us, horror-movie-style. Nicole must have peeked over too because she said to me, "They left a while ago."

"But why?"

Nicole shrugged. "Some people just like to hop around, place to place, making fun of people who are enjoying themselves. Because, you know, they're so cool."

"So, do you want to do anything else?"

She shook her head, which got me thinking that our non-date was ending, but then she added, "Erin's having a small get-together at her house, but that's not for a little while. Want to go for a walk?"

*

We strolled uptown in the direction where I lived. We were on the same route I took when I'd been pulled over by the police. A few blocks away from the arcade, right where a streetlight was out and a tree hung overhead. The darkness helped me glance at her every so often. She looked way too pretty to be walking with someone like me. I was constantly aware of how I must look to her. I felt like a character on a TV show, but all the shows I could think of would portray the date as something comical and doomed. I could have (and probably really should have) asked Dad for advice, but that meant talking to him.

A Toyota Camry, same as Jay's, belched by us. I looked for an ICP decal on the bumper.

"Did you think that was Jay's car, too?" Nicole asked.

"Probably out looking for a high school party to crash."

"What's that supposed to mean?" Nicole asked.

I shrugged and said nothing because I didn't want to seem like I was challenging any friendship she had with Jay.

Nicole continued, "Well, he won't be there tonight at Erin's. She did invite Robbie, though. Do you have any strong opinions about Robbie?"

"Robbie's okay. Better than Jay."

"Is he, though?"

"Now what's *that* supposed to mean?"

Unlike me, Nicole had no issue explaining herself. "All he does is talk about all the concerts he's gone to. *He tries so hard.*" She added, in a mocking tone, "Did you know he was at Woodstock this summer?"

"Actually, I didn't."

"Really? That's all he talks about. He swears that he threw one of the water bottles that made it up on stage with Kid Rock."

"Didn't everyone throw water bottles at Kid Rock?"

Sirens wailed for our attention in the distance. We relented to them when the sirens were upon us. A firetruck and two police cars led a school bus down Main Street. I could make out some of the players, my own classmates, by the flexing arms hanging out the window of the bus. Some of them were holding up a single index finger to show that they were #1. Others were flipping off the very town that they'd just won a state championship for.

At that moment, I was feeling the closest thing to school spirit that I'd ever experienced. It was less about the football players returning home after their latest triumph than it was about sharing the moment with Nicole. Standing with her, more than anything else, made me feel like I was a part of something, and that life could promise many more moments like this.

Nicole was smiling, watching me. "You think those guys are so cool, don't you?"

"It's just nice to see something like that. Isn't it?"

Nicole crinkled her nose. "All it means to me is that the jocks from your school beat the jocks from somewhere else."

"I think you're just mad because your school ended up with a losing record."

"That's Kyle's and his buddies' fault. They were our starters. You couldn't tell by how they tried to intimidate you that they were football players?"

"They didn't intimidate me."

"I know they didn't." She paused. "They kept miming giving a blowjob at us at the arcade. I don't think you saw. You were so focused on not crashing."

"No, I didn't see that. You should've told me."

"What would you have done?"

"I don't know."

"Well, I wouldn't have wanted you to."

"Then why did you tell me now?"

This time, it was Nicole's turn to say she didn't know. She eventually asked, "Does it bother you that guys think that when they see me?"

"Would you believe me if I said 'no?'"

"I would, actually."

We circled back to Nicole's car and headed to Erin's. We cruised through Canandaigua a few miles below the speed limit. The lazy streetlights, the early-1900s buildings on Main Street—the whole town at its most beautiful in passing. I stole quick glances of Nicole the entire ride while she hummed along to songs on the radio. I didn't speak because I didn't want to disturb her. I was happy to just be a part of her surroundings.

✶

Erin lived in a large Victorian home twenty minutes outside of town. The house was painted violet, which had begun to chip, and there was a long driveway that stretched past the house to a small barn in the back. It almost looked like no one was home because all the lights were off.

"They must be in the basement," Nicole said.

I followed her to the side yard and some stairs that led down to a door. Nicole knocked, but she was already walking in when Erin yelled "It's open," which was followed by some voices snickering.

Erin and her friends were sitting in the main part of her

basement, which had been turned into an entertainment center. There was a television that looked to be from the 1980s, thick and wide with two huge antennae jutting straight out. Beside the television, there were shelves of books: how-to guides and children's books and Danielle Steele novels intermixed with old records collecting dust. The stereo, playing Lauryn Hill at medium volume, was on the closest shelf. A couch and a loveseat, also looking like they came from the '80s, with their maroon coloring and cigarette burns on the armrests, faced the television and bookshelves. Erin was seated in the middle of the couch, a friend on each side of her. On the loveseat, by himself, was Robbie.

"Everyone, this is Cody," Nicole said, "Cody, everyone."

"Pull up some chairs and join us," Erin said.

I grabbed two folding chairs pushed up against a wall, not far from the boiler. They were caked in dust and cobwebs, but I resisted the urge to dust them off because I wanted to seem as if I didn't care. I positioned our seats perpendicular to everyone else so we were facing the entire group. Only when we finally sat down did I notice the cans of Genny Light between Erin's feet and in the laps of her two friends, as well as the blunt hanging loose between Robbie's index finger and thumb.

"So, how was your guys's date?" Erin asked.

Nicole glared at her.

The room got quiet. Everyone looked down at their beers or in another direction.

"Um, did we interrupt something?" Nicole asked finally.

"No, we were just talking about some people at school," Erin explained. She sat up and pointed to Robbie. "Did you know this scumbag had sex with Allison from our Trig class?"

"Which one? There are, like, three Allisons in that class."

Erin specified which one. Nicole looked over at Robbie, who didn't seem to know what to do with himself. He raised the blunt to his lips and took a long, slow drag. He was making such a show out of how little he cared—which meant, of course, he cared a lot.

"Was she any good?" Nicole asked.

Erin answered for him, "He called her a dead fish." She turned to Robbie, who was covering his face with both hands, "What? You did? Those were your exact words."

"Eww," Nicole said while the others kept laughing.

"Okay, guys, stop. We're making Cody uncomfortable," Erin said. I wasn't sure what I did, or didn't do, to give her that idea, but I was certain that speaking up wouldn't help.

There was a knock on the door behind us.

"Dom!" Erin squealed, shooting up from her seat and running past us to hug him. "Risen from the dead! Come sit. The seat next to Nicole is taken—"

"All good," Dominic replied, emerging into view. He pointed to the stack of folding chairs by the furnace, "There are plenty others."

"Not those! They're dirty," Erin said, "Here," scooting her friends over, "there's room on the couch."

Dominic took a seat next to Erin. He introduced himself to her two friends from school. And nodded to Robbie. He then looked over at me and Nicole, not immediately saying anything, like just seeing if we were worth a greeting.

"What's up, Nicole?" he said finally. "Cody."

"Where have you been? What made you come by?" Erin asked.

"Just wanted to see what everyone was up to—and to kill all the gossip," Dominic said before smiling. "It's not like I have to worry about school at the moment."

"Are you free to go . . . wherever ?" Erin asked, and when Dominic didn't immediately respond, she added, "So have you gotten your SAT score yet?"

"1280."

"That's great," Erin exclaimed. The others congratulated him, drowned out by Erin again as she asked Dominic if he wanted a beer. She sprang up when he said he did.

"Cody and I would like one too," Nicole said.

"Cody, I keep running into you," Dominic remarked. He turned to Nicole and added, "I just saw this guy at the mall. Hanging out with that loudmouth friend of his and—who was that with you? Your mom?"

"My sister."

He shrugged.

"You didn't tell me you two saw each other at the mall," Nicole said to me.

"Hey," Dominic said, "did you all know it was this guy's birthday recently? Do any of you know what happened to him in Gym on his birthday?"

"Dominic, your beer," Nicole said, handing it to him from Erin.

The talk turned to their friends from school. I tried to keep up, but there were too many names, too many stories, so I got lost. I interjected every once in a while to show that I'd been listening, but I didn't want to pretend to know everything they were talking about. Dominic took the opposite approach: talking as if he knew everybody, as if even things that had nothing to do with him could somehow revolve around him.

He stopped and turned to me, "Why you so quiet over there, man? You *do* talk, don't you? You *can*, right?"

"Not everyone needs to dominate conversations," I said.

Erin rested her hand on Dominic's knee so he'd look at her. "Cody thinks being quiet is a personality," she said.

With no one else noticing but me, Nicole switched her beer, now empty, with mine, which was still about half full. She drank the rest of it in a few gulps and stood up.

"We're going to head out now," she said.

I stood up with her. As the door closed behind us, I heard Erin exclaim, "I'll have to tell Jay that we had Player A and Player B together at one party! He'll find it so funny."

We drove back to my home in silence. We'd made it to the front of my townhouse and pulled into a spot by the curb when Nicole said, "How come you didn't tell me you ran into Dominic at the mall?"

"I guess I didn't want to."

"Why not?"

"I didn't want you thinking about him while you were with me."

"Cody—"

"I know we just went out as friends, but...."

She turned her face from me, giving away nothing about what she was feeling. We stared through the windows out at the world that had grown dark around us. Through an opening in the trees, the same infinity of stars I only noticed when I felt sad.

I placed my hand on top of hers on the steering wheel. I said nothing, even when she smiled. I just wrapped my fingers around hers. She turned and kissed me. I started kissing her back before she could pull away, and when she sat back, I leaned in so that we could kiss for just a moment longer.

She pulled away slowly and got out, then opened the door to the back seat and yanked at the latch that brought it down, so that the entire back of the car was flat and even, then got in. She kicked off her shoes, reached her leg through to the front, and tapped my shoulder with her foot, "Tag. You're it."

I went after her, crawled between the driver and passenger seats, almost falling on my face when I tried to plant my hand where I thought the armrest was. I shimmied up to kiss her, and she let me. She held my face in her hands and kissed me back.

"We're not going to have sex," she said.

She put her hands on my shoulders and pushed my head down to where she wanted it. I heeded her every instruction to move to the right, to the left, up a little, and up a little more, "Right there, right there," she repeated.

9 Substantiate

THAT MONDAY James drove me to school. It was the first time we didn't take the bus or have our parents take us. We entered the building through the same entrance as always, but walking there from the student parking lot, as opposed to the parents' drop off, made it feel new. Like leveling up in a video game.

I told him about seeing Dominic on Saturday. "He had things to say about you, dude."

"What'd I ever do to him?"

"He just said you run your mouth a lot."

"But *I'm* not the one who started the rumor about him being dead. I just don't get why everyone thinks I talk too much."

"Maybe you should stop for a little while."

Leaves gathered in the corners of the hallway, carried in through the front door on the careless feet of sleepy teenagers.

"Whose side you on?"

"Yours. Always yours."

"Dude has a lot of nerve. Talking shit when he's the one who got arrested."

"That didn't seem to faze him. He seems exactly the same."

James shook his head. "These rich kids think they're so untouchable."

We met up with Andrew and Eric in the school atrium.

"I bombed the SATs," Eric said when he saw us. "I just went blank during the Math portion. Same thing during the English section. All the questions seemed to have more than one answer. I couldn't decide."

"It's fine," I said. "You can take it again."

Eric nodded as if he was listening, as if he agreed, but I could tell he was too upset to hear me. "I just need to take a break for a little bit. Maybe buy a CD after school or something."

"We should do that too," James said to me, because it was a pay week for both of us and we needed some relaxation too.

I went to invite Andrew and Eric, but Andrew had already wandered off down the hallway to meet up with Megan. I spotted him at her locker. He put his arm around her, and she gently shrugged him off. Andrew tried playing it cool in front of us, but James and I saw every second of it.

Eric was noncommittal about an after-school group trip, preferring to feel sorry for himself and be alone. I wanted to tell him there was no point to that, but I was still learning it for myself.

First period, I met with Mr. Greer, who smiled wide and assured me that we had the whole period to talk. "That gives us plenty of time to go over your writing sample," he said.

I knew that he didn't think I'd written anything—which was true, but I still resented how he was making fun of me because of it. He had me write ideas down while sitting there with him. The whole time, his blank eyes watching me, only moving to glance at his Dartmouth pictures on the wall. I got the start of an essay about Guam, about how much I'd like to visit my family there. I also started another essay about needing financial support, how I would make good on the school's "investment" of me by becoming a notable member of their campus community. But Mr. Greer's eyes and mind wandered away from me, as did so many other people's, so this essay quickly became about how important it was for me to see The Rock on television each week.

"Hey, you work at McDonald's, don't you? I think you served me and my family once. Maybe you can make that part of your narrative? How serving the community helped you connect with the community and ... and ... " His eyes widened in amazement at his own brilliance. "And helped you find *yourself*." I guess he'd forgotten McDonald's was my first idea—one he'd shot down fast.

Substantiate

Anyway by then I'd already sketched a path for The Rock to win *The Royal Rumble*, which James and I felt he deserved based on nothing more than the fact that he was our favorite.

Heather was waiting for me when I got home.

"You got something in the mail," she smiled, tossing me an envelope. I just stared at it in my hands for a few moments. I wanted to enjoy not knowing my SAT score for a little while longer.

"Jesus," Heather said, "open it already!"

I smiled and tore the envelope open.

580 Math / 570 Verbal, and I didn't bother reading anything else.

My eyes scanned the line of scores over and over again, as if doing so would make them add up differently.

"Well?" Heather asked.

When I didn't answer, she grabbed the letter and read it for herself.

"Oh, Cody," she started. After taking a few seconds to think of something else to say, she said, "You'll do better next time."

I couldn't muster much else besides a head nod. Without speaking, I took the letter back and ripped it up. I felt stupid for thinking that I wouldn't have to take the test a second time, for thinking that I was destined to get a high score. Why? I wasn't owed a high SAT score—or a scholarship—despite what Mr. Greer wanted me to believe—because my family struggled financially. And being bad at sports, and not good-looking or confident, didn't automatically mean I'd turn out great at something else.

"Don't tell Mom and Dad," I said.

"What do you want me to say? They're going to ask."

"Just pretend that my scores haven't come yet."

"Cody, they'll be proud of you. You did well for your first time out, way better than me."

"But that's not good enough!"

"Jeez, thanks, Cody."

"I didn't mean it like that," I said. "I'm sorry. Could you please not tell Mom and Dad?"

"I'll keep quiet," she replied.

I wanted to leave for work before Mom and Dad could come home and ask about the mail. Heather hugged me before she left for the mall, even offering me a ride next time I wanted one.

I left soon after for my own job. The people from the morning shift eyed me when I came in. They always thought I was arrogant. I didn't know what I did to make them think this, so I didn't know how to change their minds.

One time, Dale, who had gotten fired after he supposedly moved out of the area, had called me a "pretty boy." I jokingly took it as a compliment and thanked him, and Dale and some of the others shook their heads and laughed at me. "That's not how you're supposed to respond," one of them explained, while others held out their wrists limply and walked a few steps on their tippy toes.

It was one thing to be bullied by kids my age, a whole other thing to be bullied by adults for not conforming to whatever notions of masculinity they were taught to uphold. I felt bad for them. And now looking back, I just hope they're all okay, wherever they are. I hope they work somewhere with health insurance and a union. I hope they've learned to think for themselves.

I headed to the breakroom, where Robbie and Jay were waiting, until the exact minute of their shift, to start. "There he is," Jay said. "What's up, Taitano, you stud?"

It was the first time he pronounced my name right.

"Sit with us awhile, huh? So, like, you and Nicole dating now?"

I adjusted myself in a seat, otherwise trying not to look nervous or uncomfortable. Just because we weren't dating didn't mean I wanted to talk about Nicole with anyone, especially Jay.

"Right on, right on. Hey, better you than one of those rich boys you all go to school with."

"We don't all go to the same school," I explained, realizing even as I was speaking that Jay wasn't listening.

"You're at least one of *us*," Jay was saying, although I wasn't

Substantiate

sure I was. We worked together, and our parents seemed to know each other through mutual friends, and sometimes they went to the same bars, but I wasn't sure if that made someone like me and someone like Jay the same.

He went on, "I stopped by her place after her party, and she didn't let me in. It was . . . so weird." He was about to say something else, but I cut him off.

"You need to stop talking about her like you know her. Why do you care so much about what high-school girls do, anyway? Aren't you almost twenty-five? When you were our age, we were in elementary school."

We heard people greeting Nicole in the hall.

"What's up, guys?" Nicole said, then felt the silence of the room. "Did I interrupt your circle jerk?" She plopped down next to me.

Jay and Robbie left for the kitchen, and Nicole and I got up soon afterwards. We stopped at the sink to wash up and then punched in. I really didn't know what to say, but I kept smiling at her each time she looked at me. She smiled back a time or two.

Mondays were always busy—perhaps because it was the first day of the workweek and people didn't want to cook at home—but tonight was busier than usual. We reached the halfway point of our shifts, 6:00 p.m., before we realized it. Knowing he had me and Nicole for only a couple more hours, Todd sent the closing-shift workers out on their breaks. Jay went out first, Robbie next.

During Robbie's break I was sent outside to sweep the parking lot. Sweeping the parking lot was easy enough, even if none of us understood the point. The parking lot shouldn't have been our responsibility. And who really cared how clean it was? To this, Todd would always say something about "self-respect," the same kind of stuff I could hear coming from Dad during one of his lectures.

Like always, I swept the parking lot without urgency—really just moving dirt and debris from one groove of pavement to another—when Robbie called out to me. Inside his car, the smell of his Lemon Tree air freshener burned the inside of my nose. I wondered what smells the air freshener could be masking before detecting the same elixir of french fries, hamburger meat, and vegetable oil that emanated from my own body.

"It hides the smell of weed when I drive my grandma to her appointments," Robbie explained, perhaps reading the expression on my face.

Robbie started rapping along to an Eminem CD he was playing, even mimicking Eminem's gestures. Then, as if remembering I was there, Robbie said, "When I went to Woodstock '99 this past summer, I really thought he was going to be there."

I had to bite my lip to keep from smiling when he mentioned Woodstock because of what Nicole had told me. But even then I didn't think of it as Robbie trying too hard. He was just like so many of us: looking for an "in" with people, trying to connect. Going to Woodstock was *something*—definitely more than I could say, having only watched it at home.

"I heard it was your birthday a couple weeks ago," he said, and he reached into his glove compartment. He pulled out a small Ziploc bag and tossed it into my lap. "Consider this my present. You know what it is, right?"

I nodded, and we returned inside together after Robbie played "Just Don't Give A Fuck" for me—more importantly, showcasing how well he knew the words and could mimic Eminem's defiance and anger that was probably also his own.

Nicole was at the front counter cleaning dining trays when I came back inside. I stood next to her and grabbed a cleaning rag and some trays to help her. "I got my SAT score today."

"Erin got hers, too," Nicole said. "1310. She wouldn't shut up about it."

"She shouldn't."

"So, what about yours?"

"Not 1310. Not even close."

"So what? So you'll take it again and do much better. You're smarter than a single test score. You learn fast."

"I know," I said. And caught myself right away, "I mean, thanks."

"See," she said. "Fast."

"I barely broke 1100 my first time," Nicole continued. "Now I know I'm not, like, straight-A-student smart like you and Erin are, but I know I'm smarter than that."

"You definitely are. I'm not a straight-A student, by the way."

"Why have I always thought that about you?"

I shrugged. "Everyone does. And usually I let them, even when it makes them not like me because they think I'm stuck-up."

"I never thought you were stuck-up, just awkward," Nicole said. "For what it's worth, I like you more now that I know there's more to you. I'm taking the test again in December. We should study together."

Megan, Andrew, and Eric had made me the same offer to meet up over the summer. I'd declined. I said it was because of my work schedule, but really it was because I wanted to prove that I could get a high SAT score on my own. But if Nicole wanted to study—"I'm going to the mall tomorrow," I said, instead of answering her right away.

"Wow, congratulations!" she joked. "What for?"

"Nothing specific. I was thinking of buying you something."

"Don't buy me anything."

"Why not?"

"I don't need anything, that's why," Nicole answered. "Why would you buy me something?"

I could actually feel the blood rush to my head. Or maybe it was the sensation of blood leaving it—I wasn't sure.

"We're not dating, remember?" Nicole said.

"We've covered that already. Remember, I'm smart."

"You're really not though."

"No, I'm really not."

10 Assiduous

I'D DECIDED I was going to replace Nicole's scratched-up version of Weezer's *Pinkerton*. Thinking about buying Nicole a CD, whether she wanted it or not, kept my mind off my SAT score, which was all James wanted to talk to me about the following morning.

"Man, I thought you were smart. Aren't you going to college?" he joked.

Later on at lunch, he added, "Hey, I thought of you when the clock struck 11:50. You know, like your SAT score."

Andrew and Eric were more supportive—perhaps hoping that my score spared them of a similar fate. I liked that they seemed to think I was doing them a favor. It made my lower-than-expected score seem virtuous, but really, it was just the best I could do that day. Studying with Nicole in the weeks ahead, I was sure I could do better.

James and I met up in the hallway after school—an entire afternoon at the mall ahead of us.

"Hey, you know I was just kidding before about your SAT score, right?" James said. This was his way of apologizing. We kept walking, our paces matching. We were both looking ahead at the door so we didn't have to look at each other directly, which would have made us feel weird.

"We're good," I assured him.

We saw Eric sitting alone on the bench near the student parking lot. He turned to us when we called out to him. "I missed my bus," he explained sheepishly.

His tone made me think that he was going to be one of those people that would miss a lot of things in life, maybe not unlike me if I didn't start paying attention to what was around me more often.

"Come to the mall with us," I said.

When Eric hesitated, James added, "You got something better to do? Other friends to hang out with? We're the only friends each of us has, man."

I could tell Eric felt insulted, so I added, "That's a good thing, Eric. We're lucky."

As we walked the rest of the way to the car, James asked, "Where's Andrew?"

"Grabbing food with Megan," Eric shrugged. "They didn't tell me where."

I let Eric ride shotgun. I got in the back behind him.

We took the country roads to save time. The country roads gave James the opportunity to show how fast his car could go—ten miles over the speed limit, then twenty miles over, until soon he got to one-hundred miles per hour. The entire car shook, noisy as hell, until he slowed back down.

We hooked back onto Route 96, the main road that led directly to the mall. Eric and James were talking about Megan, joking about how accurate she had to be to kiss Andrew if she was going to avoid his pimples.

I started daydreaming about what Nicole and I could do on our next non-date. We were thinking about seeing a movie. Nicole was pushing for *Sleepy Hollow* over *End of Days*. We were all tired of watching all the ways the world was going to die, because we wanted to be able to *live* in it first.

I looked out of the window, which was really a clear garbage bag whipping and riffling in the wind. For the first time that I could remember, I was happy to be where I was, and *with* who I was *with*: With my best friend—with his own car. With enough money in my wallet for a Weezer CD for Nicole. With Robbie's weed in my pocket because I didn't want to leave it at home for Mom and Dad to find and worry.

I sank deeper into my seat and thought to close my eyes when suddenly the world around me forcefully jerked—flung my body diagonally forward against the corner of James's seat, then shoved me back against my door, shoulder catching the frame just below the missing window's thin plastic; from that angle in the back everything past the windshield blurred sideways, spun 180.

The violent screech of metal against metal. The deafening crunch at impact.

Then silence.

Somehow I was on the floor, wedged in.

A taller guy wouldn't have fit.

All I could do when I crawled up was sit and watch the smoke rising from under the hood beyond the windshield.

Eric looked back at me through the gap in the front seats, relieved to see me alive.

James sat catatonic, facing straight ahead, arms limp against his seat.

No response.

I wrenched my shoulders through to grab him and turn him.

His seat tilted, broken loose at the base, but the belt harness held his body upright. His eyes were open, but strange; shiny-looking is the only way I can think to describe them.

I shook him and yelled at him to answer us.

His eyes came slowly back to focus, he lifted a hand to show that he was all right.

His words, when he went to speak, were just above a whisper, like the first notch of volume on a stereo, *"Everyone good?"*

Eric and I stumbled out, then we helped James out of the driver's seat.

We'd hit a guard rail—hard.

There was no other car. No dead innocent pedestrian. Not even a deer. Just James's car with its now smashed-in bumper and crumpled hood, a long gash like a trough down the side, engine silent but still smoking in the center of the road, facing back the way we'd come, from Canandaigua.

"You can't leave it here," James said. "Some dumb townie'll take that corner and run right into it and it'll kill him."

We tried to start it.

James couldn't stand for long on his own; we kept propping him against the side of the car. We had to find a payphone to call his parents. Or mine, because they would come right away. Or an ambulance. But we weren't sure how much it would cost us, and who they'd take more serious; who should go and who should stay.

James took a seat on the ground while we tried to decide.

A cop car pulled up on us before we made that decision for ourselves—no one called it in—just doing his rounds around town and out to the mall, uneventful 99% of the time. First thing, the officer radioed for an ambulance for James whose nose had started to bleed; we sat down silently on the ground beside him and waited for our fate.

After setting up his flares, the cop walked back, his flashlight scanning our faces again. That's when his initial look of concern for us turned to one of suspicion. The furrowed brow. The pursed lips. The forehead wrinkles deepening. "You boys sure you're all right?" he said.

We nodded and said "Yeah," Eric and I both trying to keep our voices from cracking, while James looked like he was about to fall asleep.

"And I won't find anything if I search your vehicle?"

I thought of the weed in my pocket. And of all the other things that Will, James's neighbor, might have left behind. None of it our fault. I wondered if this thing would be going down differently if Andrew with his blond hair was with us.

"You don't have to search the vehicle," I said, my voice quivering. I swallowed hard and went on, "You have no reason to

Assiduous

assume anything about us. We just got into an accident—"

And that's when James rolled over and puked on the man's boots.

*

In the ambulance they kept telling us to keep James awake without telling us *how*. Finally Eric put his headphones over James's ears and blasted *Californication* by the Red Hot Chili Peppers. If nothing else, it kept him awake by giving him something to ridicule.

When we got to the hospital, James was wheeled right in while—just outside the Emergency Room doors—Eric and I were briefly looked at by some sort of medical personnel. Doctors, nurses, orderlies, volunteers, we couldn't really tell. They flashed penlights in our eyes and had us follow their fingers from one edge of our vision to the other. They listened to our heartbeats and listened to our lungs as we breathed. Then just as quickly as they did all this, they left us alone under the empty overhang.

"Should we have made sure they worked here at least?" Eric asked.

"Only if they asked us to take off our clothes."

We found the waiting room. We called our families on the payphone. I didn't have a quarter, so I dialed 1-800-COLLECT and stated my name as "I'm at the hospital, James got into a car accident, meet me here."

"I remember you and James doing that collect-call trick a lot after Cross Country practice," Eric said. "Who taught you that?"

I shrugged. "We just started doing it because it was our only way home."

Eric looked away embarrassed, perhaps because he'd never offered us a ride all those times.

Right before his family arrived, Eric tried to lighten the mood by pitching what had happened to us as a set-up to a joke: "So a Black kid, a brown kid, and an Asian drive to the mall," and I shook my head immediately. But Eric went on, "What? You know that's how people at school are going to sound once they find out."

As he left I handed him the weed in my pocket.

"What am I supposed to do with this?" he said.

"Um, smoke it."

"With who?"

We looked at each other long enough until we both knew the answer.

"She usually has her own," Eric said.

"So offer to share with her."

My family arrived a few minutes later. Mom and Dad came straight from work. So did Heather. I expected Mom to hug me too hard, which she did. I expected Dad to say something about how I should have been more careful, but he didn't. Instead, he joined in the family hug and patted me on the shoulder as we broke apart.

"I'm just glad a police officer was close by to help," was all he said.

I didn't want to ruin the moment, so I let his comment go. Then we waited together for an update on James

*

It was almost nine o'clock when Mom and Dad decided to head home. They seemed hesitant to leave us, even though they had to work the following morning. Heather assured them that we would make it home okay. We walked them down to the front entrance.

"When are you going to hear about the SATs?" Mom sprung on me, right before she passed through the hissing glass doors.

"It might be another couple weeks, Mom," Heather interjected, giving me a compassionate look. "Don't you remember how long it took for me to get my score?"

"I actually got them already," I said. "I didn't do that well, but I'll try again next month."

Assiduous

✲

Back in the waiting room Heather and I sat for another half hour until Heather finally said, "Want to ask if they'll let you give James a message—we'll be back to see him tomorrow?"

The waiting-room nurse looked up from her paperwork when I passed her my note. "Why don't you just come on back for a minute, and tell him yourself," she said.

She buzzed open the door and led me down a row of curtained-off beds where I found James sitting in the last one staring out the window alone. I sat down on the foot of it. Distant town lights illuminated the limits of the world as we knew it.

"We're going to go." I said, "But we'll be back. Tomorrow. I promise."

James stayed quiet.

"I think this is the first time you haven't had something to say!" I kidded him. "Hey, it's no big deal. So many people get into accidents. Remember last year when Joshua Morris and his brother got into that fender bender right outside of school? That was *way* worse because everyone just stopped and stared at them while they stood there looking like idiots. No one was around for ours, at least. Eric will keep quiet about it too, I think."

As I spoke, James's eyes looked like sponges filling with water.

"They've always looked for reasons to laugh at us," James said, "Now I've given them all the reason they need." He put his face in his hands and started crying.

I put my hands on his shoulders. James didn't shrug it off or push it away, but he didn't acknowledge it either, so I leaned in and gave him a hug, first with one arm, the masculine hug that we'd been taught was okay, then I thought, *fuck it*, and wrapped both of my arms around him. "People will forget."

"You honestly think that?" The glassiness of James's eyes was made more luminous by his tears. "People *won't* forget if it's us. Remembering something embarrassing like this is easier than actually getting to know us. I just thought that it would change this year maybe."

I laughed without meaning to. "What reason do any of them have to change?"

"So we slip up once, we're done for?" James said.

"So, we just don't slip up. Ever again. Easy."

James started laughing, and then he couldn't stop. "We just got to be perfect. We can do that!"

"Dude, we already are!"

11 Nascent

I remember a slow night at McDonalds about a month after our accident. I volunteered to go home early because Nicole needed every bit of her paycheck for a new oil filter for her car, and Erin needed money to apply to Columbia. With her SAT score, she was more certain than ever that she would get accepted. All of us were pulling for her.

I planned to use the extra time to study. I was scheduled to take the SAT the following weekend, the same day as Nicole, and I promised myself I would accept my score no matter what.

On my way out when I passed the Employee-of-the-Month plaque, now with *my* name on it, Nicole made me stop and pose for a picture underneath it.

"I'll call you when I get home," she said as I left.

James was standing in the parking lot. The rumor going around school was that the car he had crashed was stolen. Eric's reputation was at an all-time high now that everyone knew he was in the car, too. People wanted to know all the details, and Eric was happy to share them. He shared everything except for me being there.

I was okay with that.

"You ready?" James said, shivering in just a hoodie. He had both of our bikes by the handle bars and tipped mine towards me. It hadn't yet dropped below freezing, but the air was sharp in our lungs. Some scattered flurries floated by us, harbingers of the winter to come.

This would be our last time biking home from work until the spring, which was when I finally got a chance to buy Nicole a replacement Weezer CD. She gave me her scratched-up CD in return because I told her I could probably get it to play on my home stereo.

✳

The same Weezer CD in front of me now, held by my son. Even broken in half, I finally did get it to work—as an iridescent roof, Scotch tape joining the 2 half-moons to the Lego home he and I built earlier today. He parks a toy car in front—"our Subaru," he says. He poses three figurines nearby: me, him, and his mom. For me, he uses a toy figure of The Rock—probably because it was the only one I kept handing him.

I post a picture of this scene on Facebook to see if some old friends might recognize the CD. Probably not Nicole, whose last post was three years ago, but who knows?

The first comment on the post comes from James. We really do need to keep up with each other better. And we will. My days are filled with hope.

✳

Back at the end of 1999, that evening after work, James and I were already becoming each other's memories, even though we weren't sure of much else in the world but each other.

We biked the only roads we knew at that point in our lives, the roads that led us home. We caught our reflections in the storefront windows we passed and spent the rest of the ride looking for them. Every storefront we passed, our reflections were right there beside us.

We saw each other for all we were and all we wanted to be. We laughed too loudly at each other's jokes and probably almost got hit

Nascent

by a car once or twice.
> "You okay?"
> "Yeah! You?"

> This was how we claimed each other.
> And learned to claim the world.
> And learned to keep going.

Selective Index

beautiful brown people (See also Guam/Guamanians) 3, 12, 41, 51
    brown boys 3, 4, 10, 11, 13, 52, 90-92, 90-100, 91, 93, 100
Canandaigua 4, 6, 8-10, 10, 25, 27, 54, 60-61, 73, 74-75, 90, 93, 96
Employee of the Month 6, 28
    Cody 95
    Jay 6, 7, 8, 46, 55
Guam (Guamanians) 3, 27, 52
    CHamoru (Chamorro) i, 2, 27, 28, 100
        beautiful brown family 11-12, 12, 16, 33-39, 36, 67, 90, 92-93, 100
        beautiful brown son 1, 20, 31, 37, 63-64, 100
        beautiful brown son-of-a-bitch 3, 13
    "Guamese?" (Mr. Greer's College Essay Ideas) 27-28, 62, 80
NSYNC (boy bands) 3, 7
professional wrestling 2, 7, 37
    Monday Night Raw 11, 37
    Ric Flair 30
    The Rock ii, 3, 7, 80, 81, 96
    The Royal Rumble ii, 81
    WWF 4
Seneca (Towanda Band) 9, 100
Smashing Pumpkins 29, 33
thruway(s) 9, 28, 63
    490 31
    I-90 9
    Route 96 88
TRL (Total Request Live) 3
Weezer i, 1, 25, 69, 87, 88, 96

About the Author

Francisco Delgado is a proud CHamoru and, through his maternal grandmother, a member of the Tonawanda Band of Seneca. His chapbook, *Adolescence, Secondhand*, was published by Honeysuckle Press in 2018. He teaches creative writing and multi-ethnic American literature courses at Borough of Manhattan Community College (CUNY). He lives in Queens, New York with his wife and their son.